Tabula Rasa

by

RICHARD ANTHONY DUNFORD

Tabula Rasa

First published in 2012 by
New Dawn Publishers Ltd
292 Rochfords Gardens
Slough, Berkshire SL2 5XW

www.newdawnpublishersltd.co.uk

newdawnpublishersltd@gmail.com

ISBN 9781-908462-09-1

Chapter One

I don't know who I am... That's not some profound, enlightened, deep and meaningful philosophical metaphor. I literally don't know who I am.

Thirty seconds ago I opened my eyes as if for the first time, but I'm no new born baby. I'm a fully grown man.

I know how to talk, how to read and write, how to eat lobster and how to ride a bike. I just don't know who I am, where I am or how I got here. What's wrong with me?

Another thing. I've got a stonking hard on. Not your morning wood. It's solid as cement.

I'm barefoot in a plain black shirt and jeans. Sat on a cheap double bed in what I can only assume is a hotel room. It's not exactly five star accommodation. Sparse and practical is the understatement of the year.

A solitary light flickers overhead as the air conditioning chokes and stutters, trying to filter air through a thick layer of dust. The pale yellow stone walls are stained with mildew and infested with a spider web of tiny cracks. The whole joint looks like it was quickly thrown together by a blind man.

I must admit the room seems familiar. I just don't know why?

On the mattress beside me is a leather jacket and a padlocked briefcase. An eerie creaking sound emanates from the en suite bathroom. Something small wedged underneath the closed door.

A clock on the wall that has just gone one A.M.

I stand and slowly walk over to the window. Feeling groggy and stretching out the kinks in my neck.

I draw the blinds and take a look. I'm about twenty floors up.

On the window sill is a packet of matches. The Hotel's own brand.

The Tehran grand hotel to be precise.

I'm in Iran? Wait, do I smoke? More to the point why am I here? Am I from here? Am I Iranian? My thoughts are in English! Maybe what I think is English is actually Iranian.

I move over to a tall mirror hung on the wall.

You can't imagine the feeling to not recognize the reflection staring back at you.

The dread. The fear. To know nothing about yourself. To have a completely blank slate.

I know what fear is. I know that Tehran is the capital of Iran. Where Iranian rial is the currency used. But who I am? How I got here?

I move my palms from side to side to check it's really me.

At a guess I'm early thirties. Not exactly muscle bound but not a twig either. Let's say athletically built. You could describe me as handsome. The hair on my head is shaved as short as the stubble on my chin.

On closer inspection I have a nasty swelling around my neck. Beetroot purple. It stings when I touch the bruise.

What's going on?

I start to look around the room. Anxiously checking for clues.

Wardrobe, shelves, under the bed.

Nothing. Zilch. Nada.

That eerie sound still reverberating from the direction of the en suite.

You know I could tell you that a great horned owl can turn its head two hundred and seventy degree's. That our eyes stay the same size all through our lives while our noses and ears grow. That Jupiter is bigger then all the other planets in our solar system combined and that all royal babies are baptized with water purchased from the river Jordan but where I grew up, what school I went too, what car I drive or what I do for a living?

Nothing. No idea.

I check my jeans and shirt pockets. Empty.

Next I try to open the closed sage brown briefcase lying on the mattress but it's sealed with a 6 number code.

I put the leather jacket on. It's a perfect fit.

In the coat pockets there's a wallet and a portable USB hard-drive. Becoming more impatient by the second I toss the mini hard-drive aside and check the wallet.

No credit, gym or business card. Nothing that has a name on it.

There's no money either. It's completely empty with the exception of two dog-eared Polaroid's.

My reflection is in one picture but slightly younger with a different, longer hairstyle. I don't want to call it a mullet but, well, it's a mullet. I look happy though.

I'm wearing a tuxedo and standing next to an attractive girl in a traditional off the shoulder bridal gown.

I squeeze my eyes tight and concentrate, desperately try to conjure up a memory but all I see is darkness.

Her face doesn't jolt anything inside my head. Why can't I remember?!

In the picture my reflection and his bride stand holding a knife to a four tier wedding cake. They look blissfully in love.

We look blissfully in love.

I glance down to my wedding finger but there's no wedding ring.

Maybe we divorced, maybe she died. Am I a widower? Did she cheat on me?

Do you know why we wear a wedding ring on the third finger of our left hand? It's because it contains a vein that is directly connected to our heart.

The other photo is of two young children. Around seven or eight.

One boy and one girl.

Are these my kids? Why else would I carry their picture. What are their names? What's my name?

Why do I know that ancient Greek writing had no space between each word and that Alexander the Great had epilepsy but not who my parents are?

Did I have a happy childhood?

Maybe the answers are on that portable hard-drive. My erection, by the way, just isn't going down. I hope the concentrated blood flow isn't affecting my memory.

Once again I look to the closed en suite door. The eerie noise still creaking behind it. I know I need to find out what it is.

I start to edge towards the door. One step at a time. I can feel my heart racing. Thumping in my chest.

As I take another step I hear a crunch and feel something beneath my foot.

A piece of paper. I pick it up.

The paper has 333-275 written on it in bright red ink.

Yes. Now we're getting somewhere.

I hurry over to the briefcase and enter the code.

The briefcase snaps open.

I didn't have the presence of mind to think the contents could be something sinister. A bomb. Nerve gas.

The case is full to the brim with neat piles of cash. More money than I've ever seen... Although to be fair my memories only go back a few minutes.

Nonetheless there must be at least a million here. Is this real?

I pick up a bundle and finger through the notes. They feel pretty real to me. Is this my lucky night or what.

In the excitement a bunch of notes spill out of my hand.

As I collect them from the floor I can't help but notice spots of red dye in the carpet.

I look closer. It's a blood trail. It leads to the en suite.

Typical!

I check myself for cuts. It's not my blood.

I gaze at the money and the mini hard drive contemplating a possible connection.

I'm gonna have to look in the en suite. It's inevitable.

I could just leave, right? Curiosity killed the cat. I don't have nine lives to play with.

I want to but I can't. I need to know.

I step towards the en suite once more. My hand rises to the door knob.

RING. RING. The telephone chimes.

They can wait.

My eyes lower to that object wedged under the door. I crouch down and yank it free.

It's a CIA badge.

No picture, just a name: Trent Raines.

Is this me? Am I an agent working for the CIA?

The phone has stopped ringing.

I take a deep breath, get a stern grip of the handle and shove the en suite bathroom door wide open.

I instantly wish I hadn't. Why didn't I just leave?!

Some doors are better left closed.

Chapter Two

Inside the en suite bathroom is a middle aged man in a business suit. That doesn't sound too bad right?

Problem is... He's white as a ghost and strung up to the ceiling by his neck with an electrical cord. Dangling. Swaying side to side and causing that eerie creaking sound.

Instinct kicks in. I rush over and grabs his legs.

With his body weight supported I quickly untie the cord wrapped around the guys throat and lay him down on the cold tiled floor, carefully cradling his head like an infant.

I sprint into the other room, pick up the phone and dial zero for hotel reception. A woman's voice is quick to answer.

"Hotel reception," she says. "How can I be of service?"

Hold on a minute. What am I doing? How am I going to explain this?

I don't even know what's happened here.

"Hello, Hotel Lobby," says the receptionist. "Sir, madam... How can I help you?"

I go to speak but no sound comes out. Maybe they won't think I'm to blame. Maybe they'll lock me up in a padded cell.

I slam the receiver down and race back into the en suite.

I can still save him. My friend... Or enemy?

I check for a pulse at the wrist and neck. Can't find one.

How long's this guy been hanging there?

I lift his head, tilt back his chin and put my own face close to his mouth to check if he's breathing.

Nothing. The telephone starts ringing again.

I check to make sure his airway is clear and start to blow breaths into his open mouth.

How come I know the purpose of CPR is to maintain a flow of oxygenated blood to the heart and brain rather than actually trying to restart the heart, but nothing about myself?

I place my palms on his sternum to begin compressions. I feel for the right spot... Hold on a minute. There's something hard and plastic on his chest.

I unbutton his shirt. Underneath is a tiny microphone attached to a cable which I follow down to a battery pack clipped to his hip.

He's wired! What in the world! Who is this guy?

I hear a click and spin around. My hotel room door is opening.

Someone's coming inside.

"Room service!"

I can't let this guy in can I?

A young hotel worker backs a food tray inside. He notices the trail of blood on the carpet and his line of vision immediately follows it to me, crouching beside the dead guy in the en suite bathroom.

Caught with my trousers down and fingers in the cookie jar.

I innocently proclaim, "It's not what you think!"

The Hotel Worker's eyes are as wide as saucers. His lip quivers, trying to form a sentence.

I rush over to try and calm him down but he's hysterical. He goes for the door so I grab him and kick it shut.

I try and restrain him but he swats me away with wild flailing limbs. He's going to escape. I can't let this guy go!

I reach for the nearest thing to hand and whack him over the head.

The Hotel Worker flops to the ground.

The nearest thing to hand, by the way... was the telephone. And quite a hefty metal telephone at that.

The Hotel Worker's head is slumped against the door, a trickle of blood oozing from the back of his skull.

Oh shit. Have I just doubled my dead guy tally?

I hear a click and find myself back on the en suite floor.

"Room Service."

I glance over to see the hotel room door opening and the Hotel Worker backing inside with my room service, having just imagined the previous scenario.

Without hesitation I scamper to my feet, rush to the door and rudely force the Hotel worker and room service trolley into the hallway, shutting the door behind me.

"Sir, what are you doing?" squawks the flustered servant.

Think fast. What's a plausible excuse?!

"Is there a problem with the room?" asks the Hotel Worker. "Do you need me to..."

"No, no, everything's fine." I stammer. "It's just I erm.. just did a... you know."

I act out a wafting motion and apply imaginary nose plugs.

International sign language for someone's made a stink in the toilet.

"Yeah you won't want to go in there for a while," I continue.

A nosey guest strolls past spying at the kafuffle. Gawping at me.

I notice security camera's in the hall. All pointed in my direction.

Try to act natural!

"Well sir," exclaims the Hotel Worker. "I have your room service order."

"My room service order?!" I reply.

"Yes, you placed an order about forty minutes ago."

"Oh, of course I did. Memory like a fish. You know they say elephants have great memories. What they have to remember though I don't know. Must remember to walk around in a big circle today, drink out of the lake maybe."

The Hotel Worker's not too interested in chit-chat as I make my awkward attempt at comedy. Yes, I pretended my arm was a trunk, and no, I'm not proud of it. Either way, this guy is void of any sort of sense of humour. He clears his throat to end an uncomfortable moment and lifts the silver platter on the room service trolley.

"You asked for medium rare sir," says the Hotel Worker. "I'm sure it will be to your..."

His words dry up mid flow as his eyes have wandered down to my crotch. He's spotted my boner.

Ground open up and swallow me.

I cut in with: "Yes, that's fine."

The Hotel Worker averts his gaze, turning red with embarrassment.

"If there's nothing else sir?" he asks.

"No that's all," I reply. "Thanks, thank you."

The Hotel Worker turns sharply and paces away, his eyes firmly rooted to the floor.

I watch him get further down the corridor and edge back to my door. Then I realize something. I don't have a key. I've locked myself out. This can't be happening.

I've no choice. I have to call him back. To be fair he's not too thrilled about returning either.

"Sorry about this," I say as the Hotel Worker begrudgingly trudges back and unlocks my door with his master key, making zero eye contact with myself or my stiffy.

I step backwards into my room while dragging the room service trolley, making sure I block any view inside.

Once safely in I close the door and exasperate a sigh of relief.

Out of the corner of my eye I notice the bedside table draw is slightly ajar. I take a peep. Inside... is a gun.

Without thinking I pick it up- then drop it as though it was a burning hot potato.

Great, now my fingerprints are on it.

With haste I march into the en suite and check the lifeless body for bullet holes or blood stains.

All I can find is a deep gash just behind the corpses left ear.

I gawk at the blood on my finger tips.

Revolted I hurriedly wipe it onto my jeans.

Brilliant, more incriminating evidence. I've made a right mess of this.

I start to pace around the Hotel room. Think god dammit. How am I gonna get out of this? How did I get into this?

But you're an CIA agent right? Shit, what do they do to CIA agents in prison?

One problem at a time. Where are my fucking shoes?

I hunt for a pair but there's none in sight. Here's a thought, the dead guy in the en suite has shoes. He doesn't need 'em right?

I tug a shoe from the corpse's rigid right foot. The smell makes me want to puke.

Find something decent in a charity shop; that's because the previous owner is no longer with us and their dearly departed have given away all their old gear.

People who buy garments there. They're walking around in ghosts' outfits given a second chance at life. The shoes of the dead shall walk again.

I'm having trouble removing the left shoe so start to undo the laces.

Hold on. I can't wear these shoes. It's evidence to a murder.

Well, murder or a suicide.

I fling the shoes to one side and start to meticulously clean every surface with a rag, trying to erase some fingerprints that could make me some fella's cell-block bitch.

I can't help but glare at the money. Like it's taunting me.

Teasing me. Seducing me.

Should I take the cash? It's blood money. But hey, this guy's dead now anyway, so me living a life of luxury will mean his death wasn't in vain. Think of all the good I could do with it. He was probably a villain anyway. Maybe that was ransom money. Maybe he kidnapped someone. Maybe he stole it from a church fundraiser and couldn't live with himself.

I assertively pick up the briefcase and pocket the portable USB hard-drive, paper with the padlock combination, CIA badge and the gun.

I'm not gonna feel guilty about taking the money. I'm not. I need it. I deserve it for all this shit I'm going through. I don't even know if I have anything to feel guilty about.

I take one last glance around the room. The phone rings and I answer without thinking.

"Hello."

"Hi," says the Hotel Receptionist. "We had a phone call from this room. Is everything okay?"

Instantly realizing my mistake I put the phone down and am out the door.

You'd think all this drama would make my raging hard on go down.

It hasn't.

Chapter Three

Briefcase in hand I pace down the long hotel corridor towards the elevators. I don't know why I took the gun, I just felt compelled to.

I hear a female voice shout 'Hey!' and take a quick glance back over my shoulder.

Bollocks, who's this?

A woman has just come out of her Hotel Room at the opposite end.

She waves frantically to get my attention and starts hurrying towards me, trying to catch up. A pretty Indian girl in a trench coat. Early twenties.

"Hey, Stop!" she hollers. "I said stop!"

I quicken my step. Reach the elevators and press the call button.

The doors swish open straight away. I dart inside and quickly prod the first button I see.

The doors start to retract but the Indian girl hasn't given up the chase. She's getting closer. The lift doors are taking an eternity to close.

"Wait!" she yells.

The elevator doors are agonisingly slow, but almost closed. At the last split second... The Indian Girl dives inside.

The elevator starts to descend.

"Jesus. What was that about?" asks the Indian Girl. "Didn't you hear me?"

"I er- No, I..."

"It's not exactly easy running in these heels."

"Do I know you?"

"Are we playing a game? I like it when we play games."

"Well the thing is I..."

Before I can finish my sentence the Indian Girl presses her body against mine and sticks her tongue down my throat. This isn't my bride from the photo.

Her wandering hands feel their way to my still-solid erection.

"Wow," says the Indian Girl. "You are pleased to see me."

She plants another sloppy open mouthed kiss on my lips, tonguing saliva over my mush like an over-enthusiastic Labrador. Is this chick trying to ravage or eat me?

She moves further down and seductively sucks on my neck.

I stop the Indian Girl in her tracks.

"What's wrong with you?" she asks.

"But I'm married!" I reply.

"Married...? Oh I get it," she continues. "You liked it better when you were still married to that bitch and I came round to play. Okay, okay. That's cool. I'll indulge you baby."

The Indian girl moves in closer again and gently strokes my neck and face.

Seducing me with her 'fuck me' eyes.

I guess I wasn't the adulterer but the adulteress.

The elevator doors open on floor ten.

An elderly couple wait patiently on the other side.

"Sorry," declares the Indian Girl. "This one's taken!"

The Indian girl selects the ground floor and the doors re-close, leaving the elderly couple standing there irritated. She winks and blows then a sultry kiss for good measure.

"Now. Where were we?!" she says with her luscious lips on full pout.

The Indian Girl undoes her trench coat and slowly slips it off. Letting it linger on her shoulders then slide down her back.

Underneath that coat is no sari wrapped around the body with a pallu on the shoulder. No traditional lehenga skirt, pavada and choli.

The Indian Girl is wearing knee-high, high heel boots over fishnet tights, with a tight see-through low cut lime green dress barely masking her silver thong and push-up bra. She strikes a selection of tantalizing sexy poses.

I get the feeling she does this a lot. This girl's got so many layers of make up on, her natural face probably looks completely different.

The Indian Girl forces herself on me once more. Okay, maybe 'forces' makes me sound a little too noble. She didn't exactly have to twist my arm.

I relent to kissing her for a moment then hold her back. I need answers.

"Now what?" she tuts. "Don't tell me you don't want a piece of this?"

"It's not that" I reply. "It's just…"

She puts her fingers on my lips to stop me yapping.

"Shhh," she says. "No more talking. It's time for some action!"

She takes my hand, places my fingers in her mouth and begins to suck. Back and forth keeping her lust filled gaze firmly on me at all times.

She then uses my wet fingers and starts to guide them up her thigh.

"Get it while it's hot!" she beams.

I remove my hand and scramble to fetch the wallet from my coat pocket. Pull out the photo of the children.

"Are these my kids?" I ask.

"You know, you're totally spoiling the mood."

The persistent Indian Girl tries to undo my belt buckle. I resist and stop her.

"Just answer the question!" I demand.

"I've no idea," she replies. "We're not usually big on getting to know each other… Well, not in the boring use of the term."

The Indian Girl tries to jump me once more but I squirm away to the other side of the elevator, putting as much space between us as I can.

The Indian girl is unimpressed. She slumps back against the side wall and sighs.

On the one hand there's a dead guy in my hotel room and I've got amnesia. On the other hand I've got a million in cash in a briefcase and some randy chick gagging for it.

"I guess playtimes over for tonight then," she says, putting her trench coat back over her curvaceous body and smearing red ruby lipstick over her inviting lips.

Compliments, lavish gifts, fancy meals. I didn't have to do any of that. Well, I guess I did I just can't remember any of it. This is getting your desert without having to eat your vegetables. Hey, I need to get rid of this hard on somehow.

Fuck it.

I slam the emergency stop button to bring the elevator to a halt. The Indian girl's eyes light up, turned on by my assertive change in attitude. Her sneer becoming a lustful smile.

"Now that's more like the old you!" she exclaims, prowling towards me like a hungry lion hunting a gazelle.

She drops the trench coat as I take control and lift her off her feet. She wraps her legs around me as we back into the wall and kiss passionately.

I guess I must be a womanizer.

The Indian girl pulls away momentarily to peel down the top of her dress and playfully take off her bra as if she was performing a burlesque routine. She reveals her big fake boobs, way too big for her slender frame.

Do CIA agents have meaningless sex in hotel elevators?

With practiced speed the Indian girl removes my jeans and gasps once she guides herself onto my manhood.

I grope away at her breasts as the Indian girl starts to writhe up and down with over-elaborate pants and moans.

This girl's silicone tits are so solid it's like they were sculpted from clay.

She grinds and bounces on top screaming, "Oh that's it. Yeah that's it. Harder. Fuck me harder!"

Am I an amazing lover or is this girl auditioning for a porno?

She's so over the top and into it, I'm finding it hard not to giggle.

"Aren't you gonna cover that security camera?" she asks.

"Let 'em watch!"

Guess I'm a bit of a showman too.

Chapter Four

Ding. The elevator opens at the ground floor of the hotel lobby. I fasten my fly zip while the Indian Girl buttons her trench coat.

We step out in unison, capturing the Hotel Receptionist's attention. They nervously make a phone call.

I'm still in a bit of a daze from the sex. Boner now satisfied.

"Hey, don't forget this," says the Indian Girl as she picks up the briefcase. I abruptly snatch it from her.

"Alright," she says. "Calm down."

"Sorry." I reply.

"What's in there anyway?"

"Just some personal stuff," I reply. "Invoices, paperwork. Nothing special."

We start to walk across the Hotel lobby floor.

"Oh, damn," she exclaims. "I've left something in my room. I'll just quickly go grab it. Wait for me yeah?"

I nod as the Indian Girl doubles back to the elevator. It's already started to move upwards.

"I'll take the stairs," she yells out. "I won't be long. Stay right there."

She briskly clip clogs to the stairwell as I survey my surroundings.

An eastern interpretation of a western hotel. Dated, clinical and in need of a woman's touch.

"Excuse me sir?" asks the receptionist, snapping me out of my daydream.

I turn away and keep my head down, pacing towards the revolving double doors of the main entrance. "Sir, wait!" shouts the receptionist. "I need to talk to you."

I pretend I'm deaf and stride with a purpose.

I'm barely ten feet away from the exit when three armoured swat vans pull up outside.

I freeze. Look back.

The Hotel Receptionist has left her desk and is coming my way.

I can hear the faint sound of screaming become louder by the second, originating from upstairs and the stairwell.

Eight armed swat police in full protective riot gear storm in through the front entrance.

"Hands in the air!" shouts the swat leader.

I drop the briefcase and throw my hands up. Wait, I'm a CIA agent.

I go for my badge.

"Keep your hands where I can see them!" shouts the policeman. "Do not make me shoot you!"

I do as I'm told. Crazed screaming and sounds of a struggle behind me.

"Sir!" The swat leader yells at me. "Out of the way!"

"What?" I reply, confused.

"You are in my line of fire!"

I look back.

A Maniac with a bomb strapped to his chest has the Indian Girl by the throat, using her as a human shield. He puts a gun to her head.

"Put the weapon down!" shout the police.

"Help!" the Indian Girl pleads. "He's got a bomb. He's gonna kill me."

"Let the girl go."

"Back the fuck off or I'll level this place!" shouts the Maniac.

"No one has to die here," shouts the swat leader.

"You shut up," the Maniac bellows back. "You shut the fuck up and stay back!"

I'm a statue. I can't move.

A member of the swat team grabs me by the scruff of the neck. He leads me to safety as the others edge closer, assembled in a strict regimented formation. Their firearms locked and loaded.

"Wait a second..." I wriggle free and go back for the briefcase. Grab the handle.

"Time is of the essence sir!" The SWAT guy proclaims, swiftly ushering me outside and into the back of the armoured van.

"This is the safest place for you," he explains. "Who's the girl?"

I try to think of an answer. Luckily his radio goes off, saving me the trouble.

"Team. Into position!" the voice over the radio orders.

"Affirmative," the SWAT team member replies, leaving me alone in the van to try and stop myself from hyperventilating.

I hear two swat members conferring just outside the van.

"What's this bastard want?" asks one policeman.

"Something about a million in cash," his colleague replies.

Tabula Rasa

I gaze down at the briefcase. Frantic shouts and screams reverberate from inside the building as the police attempt to diffuse the suicide bomber.

I slide the briefcase under my seat. My leg twitching nervously.

They'll be able to handle this without me right?! They deal with these type of situations all the time.

Damn my conscious. I can't take the risk.

I go for the briefcase and...

BOOM! The hotel lobby explodes.

Chapter Five

The force of the blast knocks the swat van onto its side, sending me arse over tits.

I crawl out the back. The Hotel Lobby is nothing but a cloud of smoke. Shattered glass layers the pavement.

A policeman runs past, engulfed in a ball of flames. Burning out of control.

I jump on top of the swat van, search inside the cab and find a fire extinguisher.

"Drop on the floor and roll!" I shout.

The human fireball gets down on the ground. I spray him with the extinguisher until the fire goes out.

He's burnt to a crisp. Smoke rises from his skin as he trembles, probably going into shock.

I look around for some help but there's no sign of life. All the other buildings on the street are derelict, it's practically a ghost town.

"Do you have a phone or a radio or something?" I ask.

The Policeman is convulsing. Foaming at the mouth.

"Try and hold on," I tell him. "I'll get you some help!"

I sprint up the street, desperately searching for a phone booth. I can't find one, but I spot a CCTV camera fixed to a high pole and wave my arms in the air like a raving looney, mouthing the word 'help'.

I try looking in the other direction. I can't give up, this guy doesn't have long left. All the buildings are boarded up. Not a soul in sight. I run down one alleyway, then another. Getting further and further away from the wreckage with no sign of salvation.

I dash out of the alleyway into a town square. Completely abandoned. Pitch black.

Everything is closed down except a small run down café with its light on.

I run over. Into the café.

A blonde woman is sat at the first table with her head buried in her arms. A rectangular bag in the empty chair beside her. The rest of the place is deserted and reeks of stale food.

I'm breathing hard and take a moment to compose myself.

"Excuse me miss?" I ask. "Hey... Hello?"

She doesn't respond. I edge closer and can hear the faint sound of sobbing.

"Miss," I continue. "There's been an explosion. Do you have a phone? We need to call an ambulance."

Still no response. I don't like this one bit.

I hover over the blonde and gently tap her on the arm.

She slowly lifts her head. Vertical lines of mascara stream down her cheeks.

As soon as her eyes focus on mine she jolts back, her face awash with terror.

"Get away from me!" she screams. Petrified.

The blonde stands and backs away. Her clothes are stained with blood.

"Are you alright?" I ask.

"Don't you fucking touch me!" she fires back with malice.

"I'm not going to hurt you. What happened? Who did this to you?"

The blonde panics and splits. Runs out the door and down an alleyway.

"Wait. Miss?!" I shout in vain. "I need your help!"

She's gone. Lost to the darkness.

I look around the café. It's a right state. Fly's circle leftovers and cockroaches populate the grimy floor.

An old television plays international news in the top left hand corner above the counter. The picture quality a mess with white noise and interference.

"Hello?" I call out hopefully. "Is anybody there?"

No answer.

I dash behind the counter and barge through the staff door leading to the kitchen.

Empty.

I search through a mass of unopened mail and old magazines on the counter. Underneath is a phone.

What's the number for emergency services in this country?

I check the back of the phone and find a list of contact numbers.

Dial and after a couple of rings get connected.

"Emergency services," says the voice. "How can I direct your call?"

"I need an ambulance and the fire brigade."

"Can I take your name please?"

"My name? It's er... Oh, Trent Raines."

"And where are you calling from Mr. Raines?"

"I'm not sure, a cafe."

"The address please."

"I don't know the street name. Listen there's been an explosion at the Tehran Hotel."

The voice of the Emergency services is calm, clear and controlled, while mine is bumbling and hoarse with worry and desperation.

"An explosion?" they ask.

"Yes."

"And where is the Tehran Hotel?"

"I don't know, it's the Tehran Hotel," I explain. "Can't you look it up on the system? Trace the call or something. A man is seriously injured and people are dead. Someone needs to get here now."

"Who is injured?"

"A member of the SWAT team."

"A SWAT team?"

"Yes. There was this nutter who took a girl hostage and they must have been called to arrest him."

"What happened to the hostage?"

"I don't know," I reply. "The whole place exploded. Why all the questions? You need to get someone down here quick smart."

"I'm just trying to get the full picture of the situation. An ambulance and fire engine is on its way."

"Right. Thank you."

"It may take some time to arrive."

"What should I do?"

"Just stay where you are. You will need to make a formal statement. Are you injured yourself Mr. Raines?"

"Just a few bumps and bruises."

"Okay just hold tight. They're on their way."

Chapter Six

I hang up the phone and wait, standing still for what feels like the first time tonight.

Not for long. I amble over to inspect the contents of the Blonde Woman's bag. Inside is a Laptop computer. I remove it and switch on the power, glaring out the window into the deserted city streets as I wait for the laptop to load. In the distance smoke drifts upwards into the sky. The Tehran Hotel relegated to the history books.

A news report on the TV blares out overhead. An Anchorman is reporting live on a location quarantined off with rolls and rolls of crime scene tape.

"Earlier today," says the Anchorman, "A horrific bloody mass murder was discovered here at the cybernetics research facility in Great Britain. All but one of the members of staff have been killed. The remaining unaccounted scientist is missing and police believe may be being held hostage."

What an awful world we live in.

The laptop has powered up. I double click the internet explorer icon then google the word 'Amnesia'.

Tabula Rasa

The effect of amnesia is a loss of memory. Short or long... No shit Sherlock.

The causes can be organic or functional. Organic meaning through head trauma or disease, with functional being caused by psychological factors.

In the background, the TV Anchorman continues his report. "An emblem was left on all the victims using a branding iron. The group taking responsibility for the killings are known to the authorities as the Vultures. A gang of mercenaries hired by terrorists to commit unspeakable crimes."

In the wild, vultures are ugly bald headed scavenger birds who feed on the carcasses of dead and dying animals, without any contemplation of the diseases they may pick up and carry.

Vultures never attack a healthy animal. They just prey on the sick and the wounded.

I scroll down a bunch of text on the laptop screen. The list includes: Post traumatic amnesia, lacunar amnesia.

Dissociative. Psychogenic fugue, source amnesia. Memory distrust amnesia, transient global-amnesia, posthypnotic amnesia, Korsakoff's syndrome.

With so many different types, I just didn't know where to begin.

The Anchorman on TV says, "It's believed that the research facilities laboratories, dealing specifically in the development of cybernetics were the main target as they were stormed early this morning."

Vultures hunt in packs. When they circle their subsequent feasts in the sky, it's called a kettle.

Although generally associated with negative connotations in the modern western world the ancient Egyptians actually considered the vulture to be an excellent mother. That's because its wide wingspan could protect its young offspring from harm. The white Egyptian vulture was the animal picked to represent Nekhbet, the mother goddess and protective patron saint of upper, south Egypt.

In South Africa the Nubian Vulture is synonymous with the term applied to lovers, as this breed is often seen in pairs.

Don't ask me how I know all of this. I don't even know how old I am.

The TV anchorman starts to lead the cameraman from the outside of the building past numerous police detectives and forensics, deeper into the facility.

There's no sugar coating this. It's been a blood bath.

"As you can see the carnage here is just devastating," the TV Anchorman continues. "The pain and suffering experienced in these four walls almost unimaginable."

You know there's a project in Nepal which is trying to conserve the dwindling number of Vultures by specifically sectioning an open grassy area where dying, sick and old cows can be fed to Vultures. Locals call this the vulture restaurant.

I click on a web-link to bring up some more information on amnesia.

Anterograde amnesia affects the transferral of new events into long term memory. Retrograde amnesia is the inability to recall past memories.

That's interesting an all but how do I reverse my amnesia? There's pages and pages of information here but nothing about a cure.

On the TV news report the cameraman is scanning the aftermath of the massacre.

"So far none of the relatives of the final missing member of staff have heard from them," says the Anchorman. "The worst is feared."

Vultures? More like bastards. These fucking gangs and terrorists. They all need to be exterminated. Wiped out. There's nothing worse. Stick them on a uninhabited island and let them tear each other apart.

You know if a seagull eats Alka-Seltzer, its stomach will explode.

But enough. I push the trivia to the back of my mind, focusing my sole attention on searching for answers on the computer. Tired of looking up solutions for my memory loss, I take the USB flash drive out of my coat pocket and plug it in.

On the TV overhead, the Prime Minister of England, with his weathered skin, grey comb over hair piece and thick circular spectacles is giving a public address. I turn the volume down.

Like most politicians, this guy speaks many words but doesn't really say anything.

The USB hard drives main folder appears on the computer screen.

Named 'RFID CONFIDENTIAL'.

I'm just about to click it open when I hear the crashing of cans outside. What fresh slice of hell is this?!

Chapter Seven

In the street outside, a Tramp is backtracking away from something.

He stumbles and falls over the trash cans once more, terrified and pleading for his life.

I move over to the window for a closer look. Two big menacing Skinheads, dressed head to toe in black, are stalking the defenceless Tramp.

I could phone for help but I doubt they'll ever get here in time.

I'm a CIA agent. I can't let this poor guy get his head kicked in.

Barefoot, I rush out into the cold night and position myself in between the Tramp and the pursuing Skinheads. With no street lamps, it's hard to make out anyone's faces in the pockets of darkness, but the Skinheads' giant ominous shadows loom over us with malicious intent.

"Oi!" I shout. "Whacha think you're doing?"

I must have hand to hand combat training right? It'll come back to me, when the moment comes. It's instinct, surely? Like motor skills.

Although a good ten feet back, the Skinheads are in no mood to back down.

"Who the fuck are you?" yells one of the Skinheads.

Who am I again? Oh yeah.

"Who am I?! I'm Trent Raines motherfucker!" I spit back with conviction. "That's who."

The Skinheads look at each other and laugh.

"Oh you think that's funny do ya?" I continue. "Take a look at this."

I chuck my CIA badge at them, whacking one of the Skinheads in the nose.

I'm a tough guy, a bad ass. I can take 'em.

The infuriated Skinhead picks the badge up as I turn to the Tramp and tell him to take off.

He quickly runs away.

I stand my ground.

"Well Agent Raines," announces the skinhead. "I think you better call for back-up."

Out of the shadows a dozen more Skinheads appear.

They surround me in a circle, salivating at the prospect of the beating.

I'm in trouble. Even if someone's watching and calls the police they'll be nothing left of me by the time they get here. This is kill or be killed.

My right hand slowly creeps in the direction of the gun, wedged in between my belt and backside. I'm trying to stay cool but can feel beads of sweat forming on my forehead, hear my teeth clattering in trepidation.

The leader of the pack approaches, but as he gets closer he stops. Still as a statue, his threatening demeanour put on hold.

He pulls out a torch and shines it directly in my face. The beam is so bright I have to raise my hand to protect my eyesight.

"Sir?" the skinhead asks. "Is that you?"

Chapter Eight

"Shit, that is you!" says the skinhead. "Fuck, I didn't realize."

Their intimidating postures change as they all move in. They're not attacking however. They're shaking my hand, hugging me, treating me like I was their long lost best friend.

The leader of the pack is Ziggler, a big bearded psychopath. His sidekick is known to the group as Bullhorn; a bulky mammoth of a man, almost as wide as he is tall. As he hugs me he inadvertently squeezes the air out of my body.

"What the fuck are you doing out here?" asks Ziggler.

Good question. Wish I knew.

All the skinheads have a Celtic style bird emblem tattooed on their necks. They each take turns in greeting me, all except one.

Enzi. A stocky brute with a face full of piercings. He hangs back and burns a hole through my head with his beady eyes.

One of the other skinheads somewhat resembles the waiter from the Hotel, only with a shaved cranium and sporting gang member attire.

"Anyone could see you," says Ziggler. "Let's get you out of the street."

Ziggler gestures in the direction of the Hotel and tells me the place will be swarming with cops any minute.

I nod, a little bewildered and motion to shake Enzi's hand. He just gawks at me with venom and contempt.

"Where are your shoes sir?" asks Bullhorn.

"I couldn't find them," I reply.

Ziggler snaps his fingers at a fellow gang member. The skinhead immediately removes his clunky steel toe-cap boots and offers them to me. His head bowed in respect. I take them and put them on as another skinhead collects the blonde's laptop from the café and hands it to me.

"Right this way sir," says Ziggler.

The gang of skinheads lead me down the dilapidated grimy city back-streets as sirens go off in the distance, headed for the hotel.

How the fuck do I know this lot? Am I working undercover? If I am, then I've just royally blown it.

"Trent Raines?" Ziggler sniggers. "You've got some balls, throwing that badge over."

"You are one crazy son of a bitch sir!" Bullhorn adds.

Enzi never takes his menacing glare off me as they lead us to a number of parked jeeps.

I get into the backseat of one and sit wedged between two hefty meatheads with the computer on my lap as Ziggler drives us through the derelict city. Behind us in the convoy, a second and third jeep carry the other gang members.

"Did everything go as planned sir?" asks Ziggler.

He keeps his eye on me in his rear view mirror. I better play along.

Attempting to put as much control and steel into my voice as I can manage, I answer. "Yes, everything went as I'd hoped."

"Why didn't you tell us you were gonna blow the joint?" Bullhorn asks.

"It was kind of a... erm... spur of the moment thing."

"Well it was good thinking," says Ziggler. "What a great way to destroy any evidence. Nice clean break."

I return a half smile as the gloomy city passes by outside. The Gang keep checking their wrist watches.

"We running late for something?" I ask the skinhead beside me.

He doesn't respond. Bites his lip.

"So what does that emblem stand for?" I ask him, referring to his tattoo.

Again he doesn't speak, turning a deep shade of red.

"I wouldn't even bother to get any conversation out of them," says Ziggler. "Not here for their wit!"

Bullhorn looks at the laptop. "Would you like me to hold that for you sir?" he asks.

I take a tighter grip and tell him, "No, that's alright."

Oh shit. The money. I've only gone and left the briefcase in the back of the fucking swat van.

Chapter Nine

I tell them I need to go back. I've forgotten something.

"Is it important?" asks Bullhorn.

Ziggler cuts in before I can speak. "If he's brought it up it must be important!"

Ziggler brings the vehicle to a halt. Enzi steps out of the second jeep and comes over to the window.

"It's outside the Tehran Hotel." I say. "In the back of a swat van. We need to go back and get it."

"I know you're a brash motherfucker," says Ziggler, "but it's too risky you going back there personally. Send one of the lackeys."

Enzi clicks his fingers at one of the other skinheads in the second Jeep. He immediately gets out and hot tails it back to the hotel.

I lean across to the window and shout out, "It's a briefcase."

The Skinhead stops to salute me then gallops away. Enzi struts back to the other jeep and we continue our journey.

About ten minutes later we get to an abandoned warehouse. The rear shutter is lifted for us and the skinheads escort me inside.

They lead me through the warehouse, down various dimly lit corridors. The walls are rotting and the place looks fit for demolition. Surveillance cameras are fixed at every turn.

"We need security too!" states Ziggler.

Industrial light fixings flicker on and off as Ziggler and Bullhorn exchange a glance.

In one of the rooms we pass, a burly skinhead and a goth chick are having sex doggy style. The skinhead stops mid-thrust to salute me. The goth sends me a cheeky wink as her partner tugs at her hair and continues to pump away.

Charming.

We keep walking. Ziggler leads the way.

I don't know why these brutes seem to take orders from me but I need answers. I won't tell them about the amnesia thing though, just in case there's some kind of uprising. The skinhead with the face full of nuts and bolts hasn't taken his eyes off me yet.

"Hey you," I say to a following skinhead. "I need you to find someone for me."

I take out the photograph of me and my wife on our wedding day.

"This woman in the picture," I continue. "I want you to track her down."

She's the only one I can trust as she's the only concrete thing from my past.

I pass the picture to the Skinhead. Instant recognition on his face.

"Why on earth would you want to speak to her?" he asks.

Before I can think of an explanation that makes sense, Ziggler pulls the questioning skinhead to one side.

"If he wants you to do something," he snaps. "You fucking do it, alright?"

"Sorry, I'm sorry."

"Don't ever question him again."

"I'm sorry boss. I'll get on it right away. She's local so I'll have her here in an hour."

"Well stop yapping and go do it. Go on, fetch!" The skinhead scampers away, bowing apologetically. I give an approving yet disdainful nod. Totally in character.

"Idiot," says Ziggler. "Some people don't know their fucking place."

"Are you hungry sir?" asks Bullhorn.

"Starving," I reply.

"I'll go get you something to eat. I know just the thing."

Bullhorn walks away as Ziggler leads me to a room. Behind the closed door a skinhead is injecting heroin. Ziggler flips out, instantly grabs the Junkie Skinhead, manhandles him past me and into the corridor.

"Why the fuck are you doing that shit at work?" shouts Ziggler.

The Junkie has left his needle behind. It looks familiar. Maybe I'm a drug addict.

Bullhorn knocks on the open door, gives me a plate of burnt meat.

"There you are sir," says Bullhorn. "Fresh off the bone. There's plenty more if you want it."

I tuck in. The steak rare and dripping with blood.

Bullhorn has found something on the floor.

"Hey what's this?" he asks.

Oh no. It's the piece of paper with the padlock combination. I quickly snatch it from his grasp before he can read it. Ziggler returns from reprimanding the Junkie Skinhead.

"We'll leave you alone," says Ziggler.

"Where's the briefcase?" I ask.

"On its way."

Ziggler leaves with the others, closing the door behind him and leaving me by myself. I wait a moment then tip-toe to the door.

Listen closely as the sound of footsteps trail away.

To hell with this. I've gotta get out of here.

Chapter Ten

I cautiously nudge the door open. It makes an impossibly loud squeak. Why is it every time you're trying to be quiet every tiny little movement seems amplified a thousand times?!

Anyway, I poke my head around the door. Check left and right. The corridor is empty, so I take one last bite out of the steak and get a move on.

I sneak around the hallways, looking for an escape route. I wipe dust from a tiny window and peer outside.

Across the forecourt I see Enzi, arguing with someone. He grabs them by the throat and wrenches them into an old tool shed. It's the skinhead who had gone back for the briefcase.

I keep moving. Try to open a fire escape but it won't budge. I can hear a scratching noise. It's coming from a big steel cabinet behind me.

Curiosity killed the cat right? As if things could get any worse.

I edge closer and open the cabinet.

Inside... is the Blonde Woman from the café. Her hands are taped together and her mouth is gagged. Her eyes widen in fear at the sight of me.

"It's okay," I say. "I'm not going to hurt you. I'm gonna take this off. Whatever you do, don't scream."

I remove the gag. The blonde is trembling. Scared out of her mind.

"Don't worry, I want to help you." I say. "I'm an undercover..."

The Blonde snatches the gun from my jacket and points it at my forehead, her face filled with hatred. "Back off!" she orders.

"What are you doing?" I reply. "Who are you?"

"You don't recognize me?"

Before I can speak I hear heavy footsteps clamouring down the corridor. Headed our way. The Blonde cocks the gun.

"Listen," I exclaim. "I don't know what your deal is, but what do you think is gonna happen if they see you pointing that gun at me?"

The Blonde knows my words make sense but desperately wants me dead.

"We'll find a way out together," I add. "But we have to move fast!"

The footsteps become louder. Getting closer.

The Blonde woman begrudgingly lowers the gun.

I take her by the hand and we run in the opposite direction.

The warehouse is a maze. We hurry down corridor after corridor, but they all look the same.

We're lost.

"You're not what I expected," says the blonde.

"What do you mean?"

She doesn't answer, keeps walking.

We pass a large air conditioning vent, covered by a steel guard.

"Hey, let's try this." I suggest.

"No," she responds. "Let's keep going."

"This will work, it's perfect."

The Blonde is overflowing with anxiety, trying to think of an alternative.

I power the vent open.

Staring back at me is a large condenser microphone with a windscreen cover. What the fuck?

"Come on, let's go," says the blonde. "They're coming."

The Blonde starts to run away. Against my better judgement, I'm right behind.

She rounds a corner into an open storage area, then puts the brakes on. Two skinheads directly in her path.

Shit. Think fast.

I tackle the blonde and bundle her to the floor. As the gun flies from her grasp, I whisper in her ear. "Don't worry, I'll get you out, I promise. Just play along." Then I look up towards the skinheads, shouting out, "She was getting away!"

They dash over and restrain her.

"You wanna torture her sir?" asks a skinhead, eager to please.

"Just tie her up," I reply. "Don't harm her."

One skinhead takes her away while the other picks up the gun and hands it back to me.

"Lead me back to my room!" I demand.

"Yes sir," replies the Skinhead. "Right this way."

Chapter Eleven

I'm back in that room. Alone after my escape attempt was thwarted.

Doesn't mean that I won't try again.

For now, I've got the blonde's laptop switched on. I'm scanning through the RFID files, taking the occasional glance back to the door to make sure no one's watching.

A series of sub files are on the computer screen: Summary, facts, figures, budgets, blueprints, data and operating procedures. I double-click on summary and start to read.

I need to get to the bottom of this.

So, RFID. It stands for radio frequency identification. Basically, it's an ID method like a card, only it's surgically implanted into people's hands. It's a tiny computer chip, also known as a tag or a transponder, about the size of your fingernail which can be tracked using radio waves.

Each RFID chip has two parts. One part is an integrated circuit that stores various information and a radio frequency signal while the other part is an antenna which receives and transmits the signal. You need an

RFID reader to be able to read the information on the chip. The summary also notes that the latest version of RFID tags are passive and don't require batteries... blah, blah, blah, blah, blah!

I don't understand?! This can't be what the money's for? What is so fricking valuable about any of this crap. It's a glorified library card.

There's a tap on my shoulder. Bullhorn's hovering over me.

"Fuck," I blurt out. "Where did you come from?"

"Sorry sir."

I close the laptop, pulling the USB drive from its socket and stuffing it into my coat in one foul swoop.

"What do you want?" I ask.

"The woman you requested will be here in **five** minutes!" Bullhorn announces.

"Okay, good. I want somewhere private to talk to her!"

"How about the basement?"

"That'll be fine... And another thing. Where's my briefcase? Did he retrieve it without any problems?"

"No problems, it's in the safe."

"I want you to bring it to me. I want it on me at all times."

"Yes sir, whatever you say."

Chapter Twelve

I'm waiting in the basement, biting what's left of my finger nails. Perched on a steel folding chair next to a big graffiti stained table that dips and wobbles every time I lean. A poster of the English Prime Minister is on display and being used as a make-shift dartboard.

In the corridors outside the faint sound of a struggle becomes louder.

A woman shouts "Let me go, you can't do this to people!"

The angry woman is manhandled into the room by four Skinheads.

Clawing, biting and scratching her captors, making the task as difficult as possible as Ziggler and Enzi supervise.

"Fight us all you want," Ziggler boasts. "It won't get you anywhere."

"Ow, you're hurting me!" she replies.

"Do I look like I give a shit?!" laughs Ziggler.

The Skinheads plonk her on a chair opposite me. The table divides us.

It's my wife from the picture only older and bitter.

As soon as she spots me across the table she instantly stops trying to wrestle free from the skinheads and just stares, her jaw dropping like an anvil. My presence soon reinvigorates her animosity.

My wife, she's not so pleased to see me. The love struck girl from our wedding photo, she's long gone. What's left is nothing but spite and hatred.

What went wrong between us?

"You!" she snarls. "I don't fucking believe it."

I tell the skinheads to leave us alone. I want to speak with her in private.

"Come on," says Ziggler. "You heard the man."

As they exit, Ziggler forcefully rubs the head of the Skinhead who had been sent to collect her.

"There's a good boy!" Ziggler mocks, being as degrading and one-dimensional as possible. This is what happens to high school bullies after they graduate. They become real world bullies.

Leopards don't change their spots, they just change their surroundings.

Enzi is the last to leave, never taking his eyes off me or changing his trademark stone-faced glare.

As he leaves he slams the rusty door behind him making a thunderous clash.

"You've got some nerve!" says my livid wife. "Who do you think you are, dragging me in here?!"

"I need your help," I softly reply.

"My help... MY HELP! Not for all the money in the fucking world."

She stands and attempts to open the basement door.

"They've locked it," she says.

"Can you please just sit down and..."

"Don't tell me what to do."

"Please, I need your help. I'm desperate."

"You are kidding?!" she continues. "You know I wouldn't get within a hundred miles of you if I hadn't been forced here against my will by your fucking bastard animals out there, you piece of shit."

Her voice is oversaturated with loathing and resentment. What happened to that couple in the photo? So in love.

"Of all the things you've done," she mutters to herself.

"Please just listen to me for a second," I beg.

She crosses her arms and refuses to look in my direction. Sulking like a petulant child. I try to sound as humble and as genuine as possible.

"I don't know what happened between us," I say, "But whatever it was, I'm..."

"...Don't you dare apologize!" she interrupts. "Don't you dare say you're sorry. There's some things you just cannot apologize for."

"Like what?" I ask.

My wife takes her seat and aggressively plants two fists into the table.

"Like what, LIKE WHAT!" she shrieks. "What do you mean, like what?!"

"It's just..."

"What do you mean you don't know what happened?"

I walk to the door to check for eavesdroppers. All clear. Satisfied, I go to sit on the table right beside my wife. She immediately jumps off her seat and backs away.

"Don't you get any closer!" she warns me.

"I'm not gonna do anything," I reply sincerely. "I just wanna talk."

"Fine, talk, just back away. Go and sit where you were."

It doesn't take a genius to tell she's petrified of me being too close, so I go back to my original seat.

With a safe distance established, she cautiously follows suit.

"Well go on then," she scowls. "Get on with it."

"The thing is..." I tell her. "I can't remember anything."

"You what?"

"I can't. Nothing at all."

"What is this, some kind of sick joke? Is this how you get your rocks off?"

"No, I'm serious. I can't remember a thing from before I woke up in a hotel room a few hours ago. I don't even know how I got there."

"This is low, Kristian, even for you."

"What did you just call me?"

"Excuse me?!"

"Kristian? But my name's Trent Raines!"

Not convinced by my memory loss revelation, I slide the CIA badge across the table. She picks it up and can't help but laugh.

"Where did you get this from?" she questions.

"It was in the hotel room," I reply.

"Are you for real? What have you got, amnesia or something?"

"I must have."

Some sort of retrograde case, possibly post-traumatic.

"Are you serious?" she asks sceptically.

"Swear to god." I declare.

"What do you know about God?"

"I don't know. Am I a religious man?"

"Ha. A religious man. Classic."

"This isn't a joke... What's your name? See I don't even know my own wife's name."

"Ex-wife!" she quickly corrects.

"Okay, ex-wife."

"How did you know we were married then?"

"I had a wallet on me when I woke up," I explain. "There was a picture of the two of us on our wedding day inside."

"You kept a photo, how sweet!" she jaunts. "So what, get a whack on the head did we?"

"I don't think so." I reply.

"Aren't you lucky," she sneers.

I check my cranium for bumps.

Tabula Rasa

In movies and quirky TV sitcoms, a blow to the head resulting in a loss of memory is usually cured with another blow to the same spot. In reality of course, this would only make things a hundred times worse. Think severe swelling of the brain.

My Wife... My Ex-Wife, is still refusing to believe the story, trying to read my face like a poker player on a bluff.

There seems to be some loud noises coming from above. Like building work or moving heavy furniture. Strangely, my ex-wife seems completely oblivious.

"Can you not hear that?" I ask.

"Hear what?" she replies, not even bothering to look upwards and humour me.

"Why do you hate me so much? What happened to our marriage? I cheated on you, didn't I?"

"If only that was why. That's a holiday in the sun compared to what I left you for."

"Then tell me. I need to know."

"You really don't remember?"

"No."

Why won't she help me. I'm getting really frustrated now. I need to find out about my history. I hurriedly fumble the family snapshot from my wallet and toss it over to my ex-wife.

I ask, "Are these our kids?"

She takes one quick glance at the photo and nonchalantly flings it back.

"That's you as a child," she states.

"So we don't have any?"

"I was pregnant once... but you forced me to have an abortion."

No way.

"You were so jealous the baby wasn't yours," she says, "You made me terminate it."

I can feel my eyes welling up with tears.

What sort of person am I?

"When I refused and tried to flee," she continues, "You tracked me down and drugged me."

Is she telling the truth or does she have an axe to grind?

"So the kid wasn't mine. You cheated on me?" I try to rationalize.

"Of course it wasn't yours," she grunts. "That would be impossible."

What am I, impotent or something?

"Who was the father then?" I enquire. "Where is he now?"

"Where you put him... The cemetery."

"I'm a murderer?"

"You really can't remember any of this?"

I shake my head. I feel like the walls are crashing in around me.

This is a nightmare. Please be a nightmare.

"A CIA agent," my ex giggles. "That's funny, you couldn't be any more wrong."

"What do you mean?" I exclaim. "So if I'm not CIA agent Trent Raines, then who am I?"

"What did your buddies outside say when you told them all this?"

"I haven't said anything to them. You're the only one I can trust because you're in the picture with me. I don't even know how they know me or who they are."

"You really wanna know?"

"YES. Tell me!"

My ex-wife leans in. A vindictive gleam in her eye and smirk on her lips.

"Your name is Kristian Alexander," she persists, "and the only connection you have with the CIA is being on their most-wanted list. That bunch of psycho's outside... They're the Vultures!"

This can't be happening.

"Why the fuck am I mixed up with them?" I ask.

"Mixed up with them..." she sniggers. "You're their leader!"

Chapter Thirteen

No. I won't believe it. I can't believe it.

"You want proof?" asks my ex-wife. "Have you noticed they all have the same tattoo on their necks?"

"Yeah but I don't have it on mine!" I reply.

"Unbutton your shirt."

I reluctantly obey, dreading the truth. With every button, more ink is revealed, until an immense Vulture tattoo stares back up at me, engraved into my sternum for all eternity.

It's there and there's no denying it. This is my middle-eastern nightmare.

"You see, all gang leaders," she happily informs me, "whether a small-time neighbourhood outfit, or a well organised world-renowned terrorist group like yours, have their emblem tattooed across their heart. It's a symbol or status and devotion. Belonging. Loyalty."

I can't believe what I'm hearing. I'm a monster.

My old flame takes pleasure watching me fall apart at the seams.

Revelling in my despair.

"You've killed thousands of innocent people," she taunts. "Slain them like they were nothing. Without mercy, without compassion."

"Don't say that."

"Men, women and children."

What have I done?

"You've butchered families and blown up towns," she continues.

"Stop," I plead.

"The misery and suffering you've caused, it would take a lifetime to just write it all down."

A repressed memory is the inability to recall stressful or traumatic experiences. This is your brain pulling out a defence mechanism to protect you.

My ex isn't done laying the boot in.

"You think that once I found out what you were really doing for a living, I'd want to stay married to you?" she sneers.

Some memories are better forgotten.

My Ex-Wife lights herself a cigarette and triumphantly puffs away.

I can feel a solitary tear trickle down my cheek.

How could I be so evil. So cruel. How could I do those things...?

Well no more. If this is my past, I don't want my memories back.

I'll be haunted every time I close my eyes.

I can change. I will change. This is my chance to start fresh.

The amnesia has given me a blank slate.

I'm not that monster anymore. The one she knew.

There's a sharp knock on the basement door. Ziggler and Bullhorn barge in.

I quickly wipe away my tears and put on the pretence.

"What is it?" I snap. "I said to leave us alone."

"Sorry boss." says Ziggler. "But there's a problem with the shipment. The driver wants you to sign off on it personally."

"Fine, bring him in."

"He's not here."

"Then where is he?"

"About fifty miles out of the city in his truck and refusing to come any closer. There's a car waiting for you outside."

Reluctantly I stand. Looking in Bullhorn's direction I demand "Where's my briefcase?"

"Don't worry," says Bullhorn. "I'll bring it to you when you return."

"But..."

"There really is no time to waste sir!" insists Ziggler.

I'm too drained to argue. I nod, ready to follow.

"Right this way sir," says Bullhorn.

"What shall we do with her Kristian?" Ziggler asks.

"Take her home," I reply.

I start to leave with Ziggler and Bullhorn. As I pass my Ex-Wife, she clutches onto my arm and pulls me close.

"Kristian," she whispers. "I wish I could lose my memory of you!"

Chapter Fourteen

I wake up in a car. My head slumped and rattling against the window as Ziggler drives the pair of us deep into the desert, the headlights the only source of illumination for miles.

You know the biggest dessert in the world isn't the Sahara! It's actually Antarctica.

I ask Ziggler what time it is. He replies, "Just gone four A.M!"

"Who's that blonde we've got tied up at base?"

"Raines's partner," reveals Ziggler. "Lucky you found that microphone before. We reckon they were trying to bug our entire place."

That's odd, I don't remember telling anyone about finding the microphone.

The car is approaching a lorry parked slightly off the road at a truck stop.

"This is our guy," utters Ziggler.

A fat grubby Truck driver waits outside his cabin. Smoking a cigar, with his other hand rooting around in his pants. Care workers refer to this act in their trade as 'digging the garden'.

Pronounced pools of sweat seep through the Truck driver's overalls at his neckline and under his armpits. He stubs the cigar out as soon as Ziggler pulls up and attempts to neaten his old rat of a hairstyle.

Ziggler switches off the engine and we step out and approach the truck driver. He seems in awe of my presence and nervously offers a handshake. I glare at his dirty outstretched palm with disdain and he quickly retracts the welcome.

"An honour to meet you Mister Alexander," the podgy Truck Driver sniffles. "I'm sorry I requested you come personally but considering the delicacy of this kind of shipment... I hope you understand."

I stay cold and angst ridden. My own interpretation of my past.

"If you would like to check that everything is in order?" he offers. "Please, go ahead."

I walk around the back of the lorry as Ziggler stays put and starts to give the truck driver an earful about dragging his boss all the way out to the desert in the middle of the night.

I unbolt the heavy doors and push one back slightly. Great, what am I, a drug dealer too?

It's practically pitch black inside.

Out of the shadows I see the whites of someone's eyes, a young peasant boy. Sorrowful, filthy and malnourished.

I heave the door back to its capacity and can't quite believe my eyes.

The lorry is filled with men, women and children. Tired and starving. Slaves crammed in like battery hens.

The young boy reaches out to me with his hand. Out of nowhere, Ziggler surfaces and wallops the slave boy hard in the face with the point of his elbow.

"Keep your hands to yourself you little cunt!" barks Ziggler.

The boy's nose is bloodied. Another slave cradles him in their arms. They're all absolutely terrified. Some of the women are weeping while others try to silence them and avoid any unwanted attention.

"If you're happy?" Ziggler asks, "The driver will head on to the drop off point."

I'm in too much shock to form a sentence.

He takes my silence as a 'Yes' and slams the doors shut. Ziggler then pounds twice on the side of the vehicle to signal the driver to get moving.

Ziggler informs me that we should get a good price for most of these and that the ones that can't be sold to work can be dumped out in the desert and go swimming in the sand.

Chapter Fifteen

Ziggler drives us back to base. I stare out of the window watching the desert flash by. Vast and merciless. A breeding ground of hopelessness as sand meets sky for as far as the eye can see. Dry and deathly serene, the desert drains the life-force from everything it encounters. Maybe this is where I belong.

Ziggler fiddles with the car stereo, adjusting the frequency and skimming through quick bursts of Iranian pop music blended with white noise until he finally settles on an English speaking news bulletin.

The voice on the radio says there is still no news on the missing scientist from the earlier massacre at the UK based cybernetics facility.

Ziggler laughs. Pleased as punch. I've heard more then enough and switch the volume down to zero.

"What's with you?" asks Ziggler.

I stay silent and watch the desert outside my window, it's landscape on an infinitive loop.

Maybe I can get some information out of Ziggler. I ask him what he knows about RFID.

He quizzically replies, "Why are you asking me? Surely no one knows more then you!"

"Yes of course" I counter thinking fast, "But I want to know how much you know!"

"Is this a test sir?"

"Yes it's a test. Why are these RFID chips so important?"

"The chip's just the tip of the iceberg. These tiny radio frequency transmitters, implanted into peoples hands, they can be tracked from anywhere in the world."

"All the major cities already have tons of surveillance."

"That's just the beginning," explains Ziggler. "You see, all humans emit their own frequency, their own current. Feelings are not just solely emotional, they have a physical presence too. That's why when you're happy and elated you can feel it up high in your chest and throat. When you're anxious you can feel it in the pit of your stomach. Scared, in your bowels."

"Go on," I encourage him, intrigued.

"When you're feeling low and depressed you literally exude a low frequency. With an RFID implant, not only can we track human beings, but we can alter their moods by manipulating said frequency. It's all about control."

"Where do we come into all of this?" I ask.

"A cybernetics facility in England had been developing the technology for research purposes but once they found out its private financier's true intentions they shut down the project and started destroying as much data as they could. That's when the vultures were hired to retrieve what we could and show no mercy."

I close my eyes and try to conjure up a memory but nothing pops up. Ziggler continues.

"Some little shit had escaped with a mini hard-drive full of data, and then had the gall to try and sell it to us for a tidy profit. Hence world class terrorist Kristian Alexander taking the meeting personally to ensure there'd be no more mistakes."

I turn back to the passing scenery and notice a pack of Vultures feeding at a rotting carcass.

"You know," says Ziggler, "If you give Alka Seltzer to a seagull, its stomach will explode!"

I gawp at Ziggler. Didn't I say that earlier?!

Ziggler can sense my eyes locked onto him, and innocently asks; "What?"

Before I can respond, the flashing of red and blue lights appear in the rear view mirror, shortly followed by a police siren. A singular squad car is tailing us.

"Oh fuck!" I panic. "What are we gonna do?"

Ziggler doesn't seem the slightest bit flustered. He calmly slows down, pulls over and turns the engine off.

"What are you doing?" I ask.

I can feel my pulse throbbing in my neck while Ziggler looks as cool as a cucumber.

Confident and in control he says to 'just wait'.

The Police car parks behind us. Two officers, both armed, step out and begin to strut over. Biding their time to try and make us nervous. In my case, it's working a treat. Ziggler, on the other hand, doesn't even glance back. He casually sits back and starts picking at the dirt under his fingernails.

We're screwed!

"Fuck, what are you doing?" I say.

"The driver get out?" asks Ziggler.

"Yeah why? They both did."

"Where are they?"

"Almost at our fucking doors."

"Cool."

Ziggler suddenly flicks on the ignition, revs up the engine and speeds away.

Tabula Rasa

The policeman dart back to their squad car and start to chase as Ziggler floors the accelerator, rapidly approaching then surpassing a hundred miles an hour.

"Dumb little piggies!" smirks Ziggler.

"Fuck, be careful," I reply holding onto the sides.

"Chill out, enjoy the ride."

We zoom down the straight road with the police in hot pursuit.

Faster and faster.

"You're gonna get us both killed!" I yell.

Ziggler brushes off my apprehension with an ear to ear grin on his mush. He can barely even hear me over the sound of the roaring engine.

I'm cacking my pants and starting to get motion sickness while Ziggler breaks into a maniacal laugh and acts like he's on a roller-coaster.

He then turns the headlights off and takes his foot off the accelerator slightly to let the police car catch up.

"What are you doing now?" I ask.

Despite the pitch black road ahead we continue to race dangerously fast with the police flooring it and gaining fast.

"Ziggler what the fuck?" I squeal. "Turn on the headlights!"

"Patience," he says with supreme confidence, concentrating hard to focus his eyes on the road ahead.

Coming up and directly in our path is a burnt-out shell of a vehicle. "Turn the headlights back on!" I demand. "That's an order."

Ziggler ignores me and takes a quick look in the rear-view mirror to check if the police car is right behind. They're bumper to bumper.

My heart is literally pounding so hard and fast I think my sternum is gonna combust. I've forgotten how to breathe. Is this what a heart attack feels like?!

"Turn Zig!" I shout. "We're gonna hit that car."

"Wait for it, wait for it."

Seconds away from impact. We're done for.

With inches to spare, Ziggler wheel-spins out of the way, narrowly avoiding a collision.

The police car has no time to react and collides headfirst with the abandoned car, flipping over the top and crash landing upside down with a sickening thud.

Ziggler screeches the brakes to look back and admire his destructive work of art, beaming with pride. 'I guess pigs can fly after all.'

Tabula Rasa

Chapter Sixteen

We get out to survey the damage. The police car is a wreck, sitting there on its crumpled roof, its wheels still spinning in the air. The driver lays motionless, bleeding profusely with half his body flush through the shattered windshield.

Ziggler crouches down to take a closer look. The passenger seat is vacant. The other policeman is limping away into the darkness of the desert, desperately trying to flee.

"Shit," says Ziggler. "Get that prick!"

On autopilot, my legs break into a run. I start to chase the policeman. What the hell am I doing?!

"Shoot that fucker's head off!" shouts Ziggler from the road.

The Policeman is seriously injured and has no chance of outrunning me.

He relents and turns around, dropping to his knees as blood trickles from a nasty laceration on his temple.

"Please," begs the distraught policeman. "Please don't kill me!"

As the copper pleads for his life I glance back to the road, now a fair distance away, where Ziggler is giving the police car a good kicking.

I pull my gun out and look down the length of the barrel, reducing the policeman to a blubbering mess.

"Please, I've got a wife and two children at home," says the Policeman.

I aim the gun at his forehead.

Is this who I really am? A monster. A killer.

"Please, no, you don't have to do this!"

The Policeman still pleads with me, crawling forward to prostrate himself at my feet. But this is what I do.

"Please, I beg you. Show mercy."

My finger curls around the trigger, ready to squeeze. Just one little squeeze and I'll take another human being's life. One tiny little squeeze and in a matter of seconds, a father and a son are snatched from this life with no return ticket. It's that easy.

It's not like I haven't done it before.

I point the gun away and fire two bullets into the dirt.

"Go on, get out of here," I tell him. "Don't look back."

The Policeman is frozen to the spot.

"Go on then!" I roar. "Fuck off. Go."

The Policeman frantically wipes his tears, pulls himself to his feet and limps away into the night.

I saunter back to the road, lobbing the gun into the desert as I walk.

No longer do I do the devil's bidding. I'm not gonna be the monster anymore. I've gotta get out of here. I've got to get away from the Vultures.

Ziggler is dousing the police car with petrol, his back turned away.

There's a sharp piece of scrap metal lying on the road. I pick it up and look at Ziggler.

Oblivious. Prone. Ripe for the taking.

I bring the metal shard up high above my head and...

...BEEP, BEEP.

A car pulls up. It's Enzi and Bullhorn.

I discreetly toss the metal shard away as they park up and exit their vehicle.

"Run into some problems?" asks Bullhorn.

"Nothing we can't handle," replies Ziggler. "Hey boss, where'd you shoot that pig? In the heart or between the eyes? I love a good headshot."

I don't reply. Ziggler throws the petrol canister away, the police car satisfactorily coated.

He offers me his lighter and says "Wanna do the honours?"

Again I stay stoic.

Ziggler shrugs and chucks the lighter into the car. It ignites instantly and burns out of control, shedding some illumination on the open nothingness around us.

"Shall we bury the other guy?" enquires Ziggler.

"Let him rot!" I snarl.

"I dunno boss," says Bullhorn. "I think we should..."

"Since when do you do the thinking? Eh?" I snap back. "Do I not know what I'm doing? What am I a cunt? Is that what you're saying?"

"I er, but I..." squirms Bullhorn.

"Should we bury him or shall we let the vultures have him?!" I continue with malice. "That is what we're named after, you do know that right? Ya dumb fuck. Give something back to the very animal we represent. You know what a vulture is right?"

"Yeah it's just..."

"Just fucking nothing, say what you wanna say. Go on. You think I'm a cunt! You think you know better?!"

It's like second nature.

"No it's just..." stammers Bullhorn.

"No it's just I'm a cunt, that's it right?!" I interject. "Go on say it. Say I'm a cunt."

Bullhorn is intimidated as I'm boiling over with hostility. I get right up in his face and grab him by the throat.

"Say it!" I insist. "Call me a cunt, call me a fucking cunt. Go on. Do it."

I don't know if he's more scared of me or if I'm more scared of me. Just what am I capable of?

I can tell Ziggler and Enzi are impressed, relishing every moment of the confrontation.

I release my grip on Bullhorn's neck and march back to the car.

"Come on," I demand. "Let's move. All this fresh air is pissing me off!"

Ziggler quickly obeys and we drive away leaving Bullhorn reeling.

In the side mirrors I see Enzi gazing out to the desert to where the second Policeman's dead body should be.

Chapter Seventeen

We drive back, not speaking. As soon as we return to base camp I'll tell them I'm going to my room and don't wish to be disturbed. Then I'll make my escape. I need to get away from these people if I'm gonna make a fresh start.

People can change. Winston Churchill used opium in collage. Roosevelt was a chain-smoking alcoholic with corrupt associates and two mistresses.

They came good in the end.

Ziggler breaks the silence. "Hey, you know what DNA stands for? National dyslexic association!"

Ziggler laughs hysterically at his own flat gag. I'm in no mood for jokes, not that Ziggler seems to care.

We arrive back at the warehouse and I get out of the jeep, making a beeline straight for the basement.

"Hey, look what I found!" yells Enzi.

I spin around to see Enzi holding the Policeman I'd let free.

Bound, gagged and trembling in fear. The Vultures all come out to see what's going on.

"What the fuck Kristian?!" says Ziggler bemused. "I thought you shot him? I heard two shots."

Enzi ironically checks the Policeman for bullet holes.

"My god!" he exclaims sarcastically. "Is he the man of steel?"

Bullhorn punches the Policeman in the gut. He doubles over with a muffled scream of pain. Enzi then knee's him in the back so he falls into the centre of the Vultures' circle.

"Piggy in the middle!" states Bullhorn.

"Maybe you didn't realize you missed?!" Enzi taunts me. "It was pretty dark out there."

The vultures glare at me. How am I gonna get out of this?

"Look what else I found," says Enzi.

He's got my gun. The original one from the Hotel.

My heart beat is racing and I can feel a lump travelling up into my throat. I swear beads of sweat are erupting through my skin and forming on my forehead. I must be turning a shade of red. Can the Vultures tell?

Stay calm, for fucks sake. I need to keep control or they'll eat me alive.

"How did you get that?" asks Ziggler.

"Found it out in the desert," Enzi replies. "Maybe you dropped it and didn't realize?!"

"What's going on boss?" Ziggler asks me.

Enzi lobs me the gun. I catch it on instinct.

"Go on then," says Enzi. "Plenty of light in here. Can't miss now."

The battered Policeman looks up at me with sheer desperation in his eyes.

A bloodthirsty Ziggler pulls out his gun and takes aim at the cop.

"Oi!" Enzi reprimands. "Have some manners."

Everyone looks at me.

"Where's the fun," I declare. "He's defenceless. No challenge."

"Never bothered you before!" says Enzi. "Go on. We know you want to."

Can I take this poor man's life to save face? The policeman is trying to speak with urgency but his words remain stifled by the gag.

"What's that officer?" Enzi teases. "Why don't we remove this nasty gag."

"We haven't got time for this!" I interrupt with haste. "Drag the pig out into the desert and leave him stranded. See how long he survives. He'll die trying to live."

A couple of Vultures hoist the Policeman up and start to escort him out. I turn and walk away, trying to act as natural as possible although I desperately want to break into a run.

BANG... I hear a gunshot.

Stop dead in my tracks.

The policeman starts shrieking, sending a shiver down my spine.

I slowly turn around to see him in a heap on the floor, writhing around in agony. Enzi has shot him in the kneecap.

"Whoops!" Enzi smirks as the other Vultures laugh.

Enzi strolls up to the prone Policeman and puts a gun to his head.

He winks at me and pulls the trigger.

BANG...! The policeman's head splatters all over the concrete floor. A thick mass of crimson multiplies and slithers in my direction. A puddle of blood I should've found a way to prevent.

I close my eyes and hang my head.

"Clean this shit up!" Enzi barks at the others.

I start to move away.

"Oh, Kristian?" says Enzi. "Can I have a quiet word? In private?!"

Chapter Eighteen

Enzi leads me down a bunch of dank corridors. It's just me and him now.

"Right this way," he says.

He's onto me. He knows I've changed. He's got designs on my leadership. Is this the overthrowing of an emperor?

As far as I'm concerned he can have the vultures. I'm no terrorist.

Enzi shows me into a dimly lit cellar and closes the door behind us. As he double checks to make sure it's locked properly, I'm discreetly reaching for the gun.

Not fast enough. Enzi approaches.

I still haven't quite made it to the gun as he steams in, pushes me up against a wall.

He doesn't attack though...

...He kisses me.

I shove him away.

"What the fuck are you doing?" I exclaim.

"Don't tease," he replies. "Let's have a quickie before we head to Dubai."

He tries to plant one on me again but I hold him off.

97

"Come on sugar!" he pouts moving in again for another kiss.

I sidestep his advance and back away.

"Wait, stop!" I say flustered and utterly bewildered. "I thought you wanted to kill me?"

"Kill you?" he replies. "Why would I want to kill you...? Lover!"

I feel sick.

Enzi closes in and starts to affectionately caress my cheek. I'm quick to push his hand away and put some distance between us.

"I'm not gay!" I state.

"Not this again," he frowns. "How many times do we..."

"But I had sex with an Indian girl earlier tonight!"

"Why must you hurt me so."

I'm stalling, trying to buy some time while I think of an exit strategy. Enzi is clearly aroused and not about to take no for an answer.

"What would the boys say?" I stutter.

"That's why I'm having... You know?" he replies.

"What?"

"Sex reassignment surgery. We've talked about this a million times."

"We have?"

"Sorry, I know you prefer it to be known as gender confirmation surgery."

Why do I prefer it to be known as gender confirmation surgery?

"Once I get the procedure done," he continues, "Then we can be together for real, just like we've always wanted."

Enzi tries to cuddle me but I deflect the embrace and move to the other side of the room, wiping imaginary dirt from my clothes.

"What," I remark, "so you're just gonna show up one day as a chick?"

"We'll figure something out. Why are you acting so strange? We were supposed to rendezvous at Zargos Mountains anyway. Along the border."

We were? I stare at him blankly.

"What's with you pookie?" he says.

That's it. I've had enough of this, I can't take it anymore.

"Look," I blurt out. "I can't remember anything from before one a.m. this morning when I woke up at the Tehran hotel. Nothing alright. Not a thing. No idea who I was or how I got there."

"You're joking?" he replies. "For real?"

"No fucking joke. Do I look like I'm joking? Am I a comedian? No. I don't know shit about myself. All I know is when I woke up there was a briefcase full of money and a dead guy hanging in the en suite bathroom!"

Enzi realizes he's not gonna get any sex. He lights a cigarette and sits himself down on an old wooden crate.

"The dead guy," he explains, "Must have been the seller. We were worried the CIA may have infiltrated and sent in a replacement but couldn't risk losing the contract. I guess you must have done the guy."

"Done the guy?"

"Yeah... Killed him and made it look like a suicide."

I'm almost relieved the dead guy in the hotel was my kill, and not my fuck buddy who couldn't live with his sexuality. Enzi goes on.

"All that money in the briefcase was for the seller, but I guess he won't be needing it now."

"Guess not," I say, slumping to the floor and pressing my thumbs against my temple. This is giving me a headache.

The photo of the two young children falls out of my pocket. Enzi picks it up and smiles warmly.

"I've always loved this picture of you and your brother." says Enzi.

"Have you," I reply uninterested.

Hold on a minute.

"Me and my brother?" I exclaim.

"Sorry, I forgot." apologizes Enzi. "I know your brother's a sore spot since he got your wife pregnant and all... You sure took care of him though."

"I killed my own brother?"

"That's when you started the Vultures... Don't you remember?"

It is believed that amnesia sufferers with a badly damaged hippocampus cannot ever imagine the future, as they have no past memories stored to draw from and construct a scenario in their minds. Did I read that earlier?

Wait, rewind.

"If that's me in the picture," I say, "Then I'm what... The girl?"

I look at Enzi as if it's a practical joke I'm not falling for.

Enzi is completely stone faced.

"Well, yeah of course," he replies "Who else would you be?!"

No way.

"That's why I'm so positive about my sex change op," says Enzi.

This can't be happening.

"I know I can draw on your experiences if I'm worried," he continues.

My legs are turning to jelly. The world becoming blurry and faint, not that Enzi seems overly concerned.

People who undergo a sex change from a women to a man are known as trans-men. They undergo a number of medical procedures from a mastectomy to remove the breast and shape them into a male chest as well as a hysterectomy, bilateral salpingoophorectomy and the construction of a penis not to mention a course of various drugs including large quantities of testosterone.

Fuck, How do I know that? It must be true.

"But I'm Kristian Alexander!" I state with hope.

"Yes," replies Enzi. "But you were born Kristina Alexander. Can't believe you don't remember that."

"I'm a transsexual?!"

"Technically you're not gay I suppose. But still. You've already had the change once so it's only fair I take a turn. You know only Thailand performs more sex changes then Iran!"

My lover's full of fun facts. Can't believe I just called him that!

"Does everyone know about me?" I ask with the pitch of my voice raising like a pre-pubescent choir boy.

"You must be joking," he replies. "I'm the only one you ever told, and your brother and parents are no longer around. Once your wife found out through hiring a private investigator, you threatened to kill her whole family if she ever blabbed. As for that P.I... Well, put it this way, he lost his cock without the aid of any painkillers."

That must have been why my wife was driven into the arms of my brother for a child. Even though I've got the hardware I don't have the right circuits.

"What happened to my parents?" I ask. "I didn't kill them too did I?"

Enzi says no.

Thank God. "Technically," he continues, "it was the cyanide that killed them."

This is so fucked up.

"So what else do I do?" I say. "Hunt down and execute blacks and Asians?"

"Why would we target someone specifically because of the colour of their skin? Something they have absolutely no control over."

I'm actually a little surprised I don't have to add racist to the list.

"You kill people regardless of race, gender, age or social status. Equal opportunities," says Enzi.

And we're back!

There's a knock at the door. Ziggler enters. I try to act natural, whatever the fuck that is anymore. Enzi is as calm as ever.

Ziggler says it's time.

Chapter Nineteen

Ziggler leads the pack down gloomy, never-ending corridors through to the front of the warehouse. More Vultures join at every turn. Bullhorn has the briefcase full of cash. Enzi discreetly touches my hand. I pull it away frazzled and check to see if anyone noticed. Enzi subdues a cheeky smile and returns to his evil incarnate demeanour.

We pass a half-opened door and I notice the Blonde woman and the Tramp from earlier, both laid out unconscious on a table.

"What are they doing in here?" I ask.

"We really don't have time for food now," replies Ziggler.

Eh?

I enter the room and move towards the motionless bodies. Before, all I could see was the tramp and the blonde from the torso up. I assumed their legs were slung over the edge. I was wrong.

The tramp has been gutted and is nothing but charred remains from the waist down. The Blonde Woman is also slain and prepped for cooking. A Vulture has a razor-sharp bayonet and is about to mount the blonde onto a spit roast.

"I told you not to harm her!" I say.

The Vultures shrug indifferently.

A fat Vulture in a chef's hat with a bloody apron and a large carving knife comes out of an adjoining room.

He asks me if I want this to go?

My god. I'm a cannibal too.

I'm gonna vomit. I desperately try to fight off my gag reflex as we continue to march out of the warehouse. Waiting in the forecourt is an unmarked propeller driven aircraft.

We board and quickly soar up into the sky. The sun coming up over the horizon.

While the other Vultures engage in jovial banter as though they were on a school field trip, I just stare out of the window in a trance-like state, watching the clouds ripple past.

The funny thing is, with so much to take in, just five simple words repeat over and over in my head.

This can't be my life. This can't be my life.

Bullhorn saunters past me bumping my shoulder with the briefcase.

I look around at the company I keep. From the homicidal maniacs like Ziggler to my evil gay lover Enzi.

The Pilot gestures to get my attention and tells me we should arrive at our destination in about ten minutes.

I can hardly fucking wait.

As much as I wish it wasn't, this is my life. I'm a gay, mass murdering, people trafficking, cannibalistic transsexual leader of the most feared and violent terrorist organization on the planet.

I don't know whether to throw up or burst into tears.

Chapter Twenty

The plane lands at an abandoned grassland just outside a city.

The Pilot says, 'Welcome to Dubai'.

Four off road jeeps are waiting to transport us to the meeting point.

The vehicles travel in singular formation along Jumeirah beach, and across a private curving beach to the artificial island that houses a luxury hotel called the Burj Al Arab. The hotel is shaped like a humongous boat sail and must be over a thousand feet tall.

Ignoring the hotel's parking system, we leave the Jeeps outside and advance to the entrance.

Meeting us at the door is an immaculately dressed client liaison.

Your typical 'yes man' career type. Eager to please, like a puppy dropping slippers at your feet.

"It's a pleasure to make you acquaintance," says the Liaison. "Right this way please. My client is waiting and eager to do business."

He escorts us through the lobby, past gawking high society members of the prawn sandwich club, spellbound at the sight of a leather clad gang of skinheads in their five star V.I.P retreat.

"I trust you had a pleasant journey?" asks the Liaison.

I don't even bother to respond and be polite, staying bitterly cold and emotionless. I'm not interested in making small-talk. I just wanna get this over with. Another day and another lowlife to meet. What scum-of-the-earth associate is waiting for me now?!

The Liaison shrewdly whisks us past a number of security guards in full riot gear. We continue around a circular walkway, headed for a glass boardroom hosting a group of suit and ties, protected by even more heavily armed security.

In the centre of the group facing in the opposite direction stands a man with a grey comb over hair piece. As we get closer he turns around.

My world seems to go into slow motion as I recognize the client's features. That grey comb over hair piece, weathered skin and thick circular framed spectacles.

It's the Prime Minister of England from the earlier TV report.

Holy shit.

I stop dead in my tracks and tell the Liaison I need to take a piss. Before he can come up with a rebuttal I'm striding to the men's room and closing the door behind me. The Vultures exchanging dumbfounded looks.

I'm now alone with my hands rested on the marble sink and the reflection I don't recognize staring back at me in the mirror. The face staring back is of a vile, remorseless killer.

A sick, unrelenting and diabolical psychopathic monster of a human being.

My blood is boiling over as I remove the gun from my pocket.

"Fuck you. Fuck you!" I shout at my reflection. "Fuck you ya sick fucking cunt."

I point the gun at the face in the mirror. I don't want to be a part of this world and this world shouldn't have to put up with me.

I've done too much harm to start over. Caused too much damage to make amends. Ruined too many lives. The planet's better off without me. I don't deserve a second chance. A blank slate. I'm gonna do the world a favour.

I plant the gun deep inside my mouth at an angle that will blow my twisted brain out of the back of my skull.

I close my eyes. My finger poised on the trigger, ready to squeeze.

Richard Anthony Dunford

Some things are better left forgotten.

All of a sudden the bathroom walls come apart. Six meatheads in matching brown polo shirts storm inside and haul me off my feet.

The gun flies from my grip as the men overpower and restrain me.

They put thick electrical tape over my mouth and a black hood over my head to plunge my world into darkness.

Now what?! Am I being abducted by a rival gang or something?

I can feel myself being carried down countless flights of stairs.

I struggle to get free but it's fruitless, there's just too many of them.

I feel myself being manhandled onto a chair. The faint sound of a hundred murmurs in stereo surround sound.

The hood is removed and the electrical tape ripped free. I'm instantly blinded by glaringly bright lights. A barrage of fluorescent causing my eyes to squint and re-adjust.

My retinas are working overtime to send me an image, but once they do, I still can't quite believe what I'm seeing.

Directly opposite me are bleachers packed solid with members of a studio audience.

Clapping, smiling and cheering enthusiastically.

All wolf whistles and screams. They rise to their feet for a standing ovation. All eyes on me.

Is my mind playing tricks on me? Have I finally gone mad?

Chapter Twenty One

Mounted cameras on dollies and cranes whiz into position. Crew members with clipboards and earpieces rush around like headless chickens.

A runner fixes a microphone to my lapel while a make-up artist touches up my pale faced complexion, poking me in the eye with a brush.

It's hard to put it into words when you're lost for words.

To say I'm in shock is the understatement of the fucking year.

I'm practically a mannequin right now. I catch a glimpse of myself in a monitor next to the auto cue machine. I've got this goofy teeth and eyes smile locked on my face, almost as though I've had an overdose of botex and all my facial muscles have gone permanently solid.

I look like a right James Blunt.

The studio audience has re-taken their seats. They point at me and chat excitedly, too many voices at once to become comprehensible.

To my immediate left, a floor manager gets the go ahead from the gallery and bellows, "Go titles in five, four, three..."

He counts the remaining seconds down with his fingers and starts clapping to cue the audience. Like a bunch of sheep, they follow his lead and begin to cheer frenetically.

Theme music blares from the studio speakers as a crane-mounted camera swings over the audience, headed to a set of double doors immersed in a display of plasma television screens, all displaying an animated graphic that says: Tabula Rasa.

They open on cue and through a flood of smoke and laser lights walks a man. Suited and booted. Probably late fifties, but he's had enough plastic surgery to look forty. His skin is orange from fake tan abuse, and he has a classic Hollywood square jaw and platinum silver gelled-back hair.

The crowd goes nuts for the geezer as he saunters onto stage, overflowing with arrogance and charisma.

"Welcome back to Tabula Rasa," echoes a voice in the rafters.

"Here is your host..." the voice continues, pausing for dramatic effect, "Max Masters."

The crowd go bananas. Max soaks up the over-enthusiastic adulation and moves over to me, centre stage.

"Wasn't he great ladies and gentlemen?" asks Max Masters.

The crowd cheer.

"Come on, you can do better then that!" he prompts, hamming it up big time with his phoney showbiz chops in overdrive.

The audience respond like lemmings. An awkward smile rises in my gob. I don't think I've blinked once yet. What the fuck is this?!

"Would you look at his face?" teases the host. "He's in shock."

The crowd burst into laughter. Max Masters tries to quieten them down, although in fake hysterics himself, the big cheesy show-off.

"What's..." I stutter.

"...What's going on?" he interjects. "Always the same question. Well, my friend, you're the star of Tabula Rasa. Your very own reality television show!"

"What are..."

"...You talking about?" Max cuts in once more.

Tabula Rasa

This finishing off each others' sentences shtick is getting old fast.

"Kristian," says Max. "It's time for a history lesson. Roll VT."

The lights revolve and change into a lowered spotlight. Max comes around behind me and spins me in the direction of the large plasma screens, massaging my shoulders with his overgrown mitts.

The live feed condenses into a tiny box in the bottom left hand corner as a pre-edited segment begins.

A woman speaks in a by-the-numbers commercial vocal artist tone.

She's doused in bargain basement reverb to give her that space aged futuristic feel.

"Two years ago," the voice over begins, "host and executive producer Max Masters came up with an innovative reality show concept."

Archive footage comes up on screen, starring yours truly. Bright eyed and bushy tailed, I'm being measured for wardrobe, getting a vulture tattoo, having my head shaved and being given injections by a medical team.

All happy as Larry.

"Contestants are given a drug induced state of amnesia," continues the voice-over lady, "and then told a series of extreme revelations about their fictitious past. Starting off with a carefully measured dose of a 2'-halogenated benzodiazepine, more specifically midazolam flunitrazepam, scopolamine and propofol, contestants are now left in a state of amnesia with absolutely no memories of their own life."

While attentively kneading out the knots in my trapezium, Max leans into my ear and says, "A common side effect of the drugs is a sustained erection. You sure made good use of that didn't you son?"

I shove his hand away as Max sniggers. A twinkle gleams in his eye as he sees himself come up in the video package. He's being interviewed and has been no doubt painstakingly lit by a team of under-appreciated cinematographers to exaggerate his bone structure.

"It's really a study of human behaviour," says Max the rerun, with his real life version next to me mouthing the words. "To see how they react to the news. It's part scientific experiment, part reality television show. This is cutting edge entertainment."

The video package cuts to a second interview. This time it's me looking like a kid at Christmas.

"I can't wait to get started," says me on screen. "I hope I can be as entertaining as the last guy".

"What do you think they've got in store for you?" asks an off-screen interviewer.

"I don't know... A car chase would be cool. A gunfight would be awesome."

What a twat!

The audiences applause is cued once more by the floor manager as the lights come up and all camera's are directed on myself and Max.

"So, what do you think?" smiles Max.

"This has all been a TV show?" I ask.

"One hell of a TV show!" he beams. "The best yet!"

"I'm not really a gay, mass murdering, people trafficking, transsexual cannibalistic leader of a terrorist faction?"

"Of course not... Come on, could that ever really happen anywhere but on TV?!"

I guess it does sound kinda ridiculous.

A highlight reel plays on the plasma screen. I see myself from hidden camera angles waking up in the hotel room and opening the briefcase of money. Then trying to resuscitate the dead guy in the en suite.

"The corpse was a prosthetic dummy!" says Max. "Brownie points for trying to bring him back to life though. The engineers got a good laugh out of that backstage."

Next up I'm in the elevator with the Indian Girl's legs wrapped around me and gyrating like there was no tomorrow. Our modesty has been obscured with some well placed blurred out pixels.

Then I'm outside the hotel lobby being ushered into the back of the SWAT van. The camera angle stays wide as a bunch of crew rush in and help to topple the swat van over as the Hotel Lobby explodes.

They creep off set the moment the smoke clears, just in time for me to crawl out, completely oblivious.

Finally I'm in the desert with the Policeman on his knees and begging for his life. Shot using night vision cameras. In the clip, I let the Policeman leave and toss away the gun.

Watching it back on screen, it doesn't have anywhere near the intensity I felt at the time.

This is what happens when a bunch of TV executives, with enough stroke to produce whatever they think will bump their ratings, watch the Truman show while snorting cocaine.

"Don't feel bad Kristian," says Max. "It's not just about being gullible. Easily led. No expense was spared to make the environment believable. Some of the **industries** finest worked on this project. It's what's known as confabulation. When the brain forms false memories and perceptions from the environment and predicament it finds itself in. Once the drugs have chemically induced a blank canvas for us we have the opportunity to completely mould your past and see how you'll react to the terrible discoveries we create."

This does sound strangely familiar.

"The medication was injected under expert medical supervision." says Max. "This isn't brain damage. You're a fully functional adult retaining all your education and motor skills. You just have no knowledge of your own life."

"This is unbelievable." I say.

"I know what a great show right?" Max replies.

"When will my memory come back? I mean, my real memories?"

"It'll all come flooding back soon with no side effects. Just drink lots of liquids. Everything about this is one hundred percent safe."

"Safe?!" I exclaim. "I almost killed myself..."

"Almost," he fires back. "That's the key word there. Safety professionals were on hand at every moment to step in. All the guns fired blanks and every stunt was performed by a professional. You were never in any real danger."

Max looks to camera and says "Remember, don't try this at home!"

The audience hang on his every word. I wanna reach out and wring his fucking neck.

"This is..." I begin.

"Fantastic!" Max Interrupts before I can criticise. "Now, the show wouldn't be anything without our brilliant cast of actors. I think you'll recognize this lot Kristian!"

Chapter Twenty Two

Theme music plays as the plasma screen doors slide back. Walking out in a neat line to form a row across the stage, stands everyone from the Prime Minister, the Slaves out of costume, my ex Wife, the Policeman who had been shot, the maniac suicide bomber, the Indian slut from the elevator and the Vultures. All decked out in fancy suits like proper thespians with big Cheshire cat 'we-fooled-you' grins on their mugs.

The Blonde Woman and Tramp carry their mutilated prosthetic doubles, obvious fakes under the harsh studio lights.

Max Masters puts his arm around one of the Vultures and holds up a Channel Eighteen branded microphone. Out of the moment it's as plain as day that this Vulture had also been the hotel worker who'd brought me room service at the start.

"A big thumbs up to Brad here!" says Max Masters. "He stepped in to play a second role when the original actor called in sick. What do you think of the new haircut Brad?"

"My head's a bit cold!" he jokes, basking in the spotlight.

"We thought at one point it would have completely messed up the episode but Kristian here didn't seem to notice!" taunts Max.

The Audience laugh. Loving every minute. You know when you wonder whether people are laughing at you or with you... Well, this isn't one of those moments.

"Okay," says Max. "Let's reunite our number one contestant with some of his biggest fans. Ladies and gentleman... The family!"

The crowd cheer as three strangers run towards me. The voice over in the sky announces this is my real life Mother, Father, Sister and Girlfriend.

Three of them are all over me with elated smiles and hugs while the fourth, a girl in her early twenties, hangs back, not caught up in the merriment. This girl looks like she has the weight of the world on her shoulders.

Max Masters turns to camera and tells the audience at home we're going to commercial.

The floor manager gives everyone the all clear. Max heads backstage to have his hair and make up re-touched while stage crew swiftly bring in a podium and a pyrotechnic rig.

My real life Dad pats me on the back. I don't recognize him. Not even slightly.

"Fantastic show, son." he beams with pride. "Bloody brilliant."

"You were great as always sweetheart!" says the Mum.

As always?

A dolled up WAG coils her arms around me and sticks her tongue down my throat. I'm hoping this is my Girlfriend and not my Sister.

"That's to remind you of how good I am!" she pouts, staring daggers at the actress who played my sexual conquest in the elevator.

"Hey," shrugs the actress. "Sex scenes pay double, it's just acting!"

"Don't you forget it!" my girly-friend snaps back.

The Indian girl grabs her boobs and boasts, "These babies have just been paid off!"

Her parents must be so proud.

I ask my real life Mother, how come I don't remember any of you?

"Don't worry munchkin," she reassures. "It'll all come back. You're doing a great job."

I start to walk across the stage to meet the line of giddy cast members. They each wait their turn to shake my hand. I feel a bit like the royal guest on cup final day meeting the teams.

I get to the actors who had played the roles of Enzi and Ziggler.

"A pleasure working with you Kristian," says Enzi in a posh British accent.

"Hope we weren't too tough on ya mate?!" says Ziggler. Suddenly a native Aussie.

"These characters can get frightfully intense," Enzi interjects.

"I've gotta ask," the Prime Minister intervenes. "You didn't think it was strange that you were in Iran yet everyone spoke English?"

I let out a brief false laugh. You don't know how much I wanna punch this guy in the face right now.

The floor Manager shouts, "Sixty seconds everyone!" through a megaphone.

Production assistants pester everyone into position as my real life Mum pushes my subdued sister in my direction.

"Go on," she encourages. "Say something to your brother!"

"Twenty seconds!" declares the Floor manager.

My sister steps closer and gives me a hug. Although her touch is soft I can feel her hands are trembling.

She brings her face up close to the side of my head and whispers in my ear.

"Run!"

Chapter Twenty Three

Her words make the hairs on the back of my neck stand up straight.

Max Masters swaggers back onto the set. The floor manager counts us down and we're back live.

"Good luck old chap!" says Enzi as a production runner pulls my sister away.

Theme music plays and the Tabula Rasa logo graphic appears on the monitors.

"Welcome back to the final part of tonight's show," says Max, draping his arm around me and ushering me into position.

I can't take my eyes off my sister, her face awash with anguish.

"We have one final surprise for you Kristian," says Max.

Two gorgeous models strut onto the stage with the briefcase. They pose with permanent smiles, getting a 'woooooooo' reaction from the studio audience.

"The precious briefcase!" exclaims Max. "One million pounds in cash. I'm sure you remember the combination?"

I tap in the numbers and the briefcase snaps open. A floodlight appears from above to illuminate the money.

"Congratulations!" says Max. "What are you gonna spend the money on?"

"Hmmm!" I reply sarcastically. "Hire a hypnotist to forget this nightmare?!"

"You are funny," giggles Max. "A hypnotist to forget, how ironic. No wonder you've been such great entertainment!"

I lean in close to Max and quietly say through gritted teeth, "Do you know how much I'm gonna sue you!"

Max fakes a laugh to the audience, pretending I said something funny.

"Sue me for what?" he replies, carefully making sure his lapel mic is covered and turning his head at an angle to deceive any lip readers.

"You can't treat people like this!" I state.

Max Masters drops his happy public persona, turns to me with a devilish gleam in his glare.

"Don't try and get smart with me," he snarls. "You volunteered!"

"I what?"

"You came to us Kristian. All contestants on this show are volunteers. You signed a contract. I own your arse."

"I don't remember that!"

"Guess you'll just have to take my word for it eh?!"

Max Masters winks and swivels around to face his adoring public.

"Ladies and gentlemen, boys and girls, children of all ages," says Max. "You have been watching Tabula Rasa. The highest rated show on network television. Let's hear it for the star of the show. Our greatest ever contestant and a brand new millionaire... Kristian Alexander!"

The Models hand me the briefcase full of cash and each give me a kiss on the cheek. The crowd erupts with wild cheering as cast members jump up and down and embrace. Fireworks explode and ticker tape falls from the studio ceiling, glittering in the air to a soundtrack of triumphant music.

Through the revellers I spot my sister. Tears streaming down her face. The viewers at home could think these are tears of joy I guess... Only we know otherwise.

"Thank you for watching!" shouts Max over the commotion. "Tune in again later tonight for the start of a new journey. Same channel. Same place. You wouldn't dare miss it. I'm Max Masters and this is Tabula Rasa!"

Credit music rolls as the party continues. The second that the floor manager announces we're off the air, Max Masters drops the guise and storms backstage with an entourage of production assistants.

I ditch the briefcase and start to shove my way through the crowd, heading for the exit.

Someone clutches onto my arm. It's the actor who played Ziggler.

"I'm sorry Kristian," he says. "I can't let you go mate."

The studio audience stampede onto the stage, hunting to get their souvenirs autographed. Bullhorn takes my other arm and he and Ziggler start to escort me backstage, smiling and waving to the fans. I try and pick out my sister through the mass of people but it's chaos.

As soon as we're backstage Ziggler and Bullhorn pass me over to three waiting security guards. I struggle to get free as they haul me off my feet and drag me down the corridor.

"Don't hurt him!" says Ziggler.

"What are you doing?!" I scream. "The show's over!"

Max Masters is waiting at the end of the corridor.

"This is just the beginning," he smirks. "You're gonna make me a billionaire!"

The security guards carry me into a laboratory and strap me to a hospital bed.

A doctor has a syringe full of a black serum prepped and ready. "Are you sure about this mister Masters?" asks the Doctor.

Max Masters trains his iron hard eyes on the doctor. Intimidated, the Doctor quickly loses his nerve and injects the syringe into my neck.

"Why are you doing this?" I ask.

"Just show-business kid!" Max replies.

"The formula should take effect in a couple of minutes sir," sighs the Doctor.

"Perfect" smiles Max.

"You bastards, you're drugging me again?!" I exclaim, starting to feel woozy.

"Sorry for the man handling back there stud," says Max. "We can't have the star of the show going AWOL on us now can we?!"

"Mr. Masters," the Doctor speaks up. "I'm concerned. I don't know how much more of this his brain can take.

When we developed this formula we only tested it for one show. He's on his..."

"I know how many shows he's done!" snaps Max. "I didn't ask for your opinion Doc. Keep your mouth shut and do your job and I won't erase you from my Christmas card list, how's that sound?!"

The Doctor shrivels and hangs his head.

"He volunteered," continues Max. "He knows the risks. If it doesn't work, double the dosage. Until the ratings dip he's my star alright. You don't mind, do you Kristian?"

The room's spinning. My body feels weightless. Like I'm floating.

"Let me go!" I slur.

"You don't want that," says Max. "Not the real you. You're confused. I know what you really want."

Max pulls up a chair and sits by my bedside.

"You wanted to be a star, remember?" Max continues. "This is all you ever dreamed of. To be famous. To be loved by millions. I gave you that and this is how you thank me. Where's the gratitude?!"

My eyes are trying to close. I must stay awake.

"Please," I beg. "Just let me go."

"Before you the reality format was stale," continues Max ignoring my plea. "Plus it wasn't really reality TV. You made reality real. All those shows sticking a camera in someone's face. Celebrities making themselves look like cunts to get back in the public eye, or nobodies trying to get notoriety without any actual talent. Even if it's a so called 'fly on the wall', they don't act naturally. They act up. It's real people pretending to be real. As far as I'm concerned, it's only true reality TV if the subject doesn't know they're being filmed. Hidden camera is the only way to go, no matter how elaborate or unelaborated you want to make it. Depends on your imagination and your budget."

I shake my head in dismay. What have I gotten myself into?

"You Kristian?" says Max. "You're real. That's why the audience connects with you. You don't want to let them down?! Your fans?"

"I want out!" I exclaim, my strength evaporating by the second.

"Don't worry," Max replies. "In a few minutes, you'll forget all this ever happened."

"I won't forget. I'll never forget!"

"Keep telling yourself that."

The Doctor checks my vital signs and shines a torch in my eyes.

"Any moment now Max," says the Doctor.

Max stands, ready to leave. I can only just about make out his basic outline now, his features are all blurry.

"You know," he says. "Every time you try and escape. Every single time without fail and always in the same direction. Fascinating."

With my last gasp of energy I blurt out Max's name to get his attention.

"You listen to me Max Masters!" I declare with determination. "I won't forget this. I'm gonna make you pay for what you've done to me!"

Max just laughs.

"That's what you said last time!" he taunts. "Get him on set!"

Max exits, leaving me fading fast.

"I won't forget!" I say. "I'll never forget!"

Chapter Twenty Four

I don't know who I am... That's not some profound, enlightened, deep and meaningful philosophical metaphor. I literally don't know who I am.

Thirty seconds ago I opened my eyes as if for the first time, but I'm no new born baby. I'm a fully grown man.

I know how to talk, how to read and write, how to eat lobster and how to ride a bike. I just don't know who I am, where I am or how I got here. What's wrong with me? I must have amnesia.

Another thing. I've got a stonking hard on. Not your morning wood.

It's as solid as cement.

I'm barefoot in a plain black shirt and jeans. Sat on a cheap double bed in what I can only assume is a hotel room. It's not exactly five star accommodation. Sparse and practical is the understatement of the year.

A solitary light flickers overhead as the air conditioning chokes and stutters, trying to filter air through a thick layer of dust.

The pale yellow stone walls are stained with mildew and infested with a spider web of tiny cracks.

Tabula Rasa

On the mattress beside me is a leather jacket and a padlocked briefcase. An eerie creaking sound emanates from the en suite bathroom with something small wedged underneath the closed door.

I must admit this room seems familiar. I just don't know why?

Chapter Twenty Five

Max Masters strides through the television studio complex. His entourage struggle to keep up, all vying for a moment of his time.

A pimple faced runner is first to chime in. "You had a call from Downing Street Mr. Masters," he says.

"What did they want?" replies Max, as a caterer hands him a cappuccino and a Danish pastry.

"They want to know whether we can edit out all of the information about the RFID plot line?"

"No we fucking can't. This is a live show."

Max takes a bite out of his pastry and scrunches up his face in revulsion. He lobs the Danish at a passing by crew member to dispose of.

Never stopping, always on the move.

His curiosity heightened Max Masters asks the runner 'Why?'

"They said something about implementing RFID into National Security," he replies.

"They can't do that!" a production assistant butts in. "There'd be riots in the streets!"

"You underestimate the power of TV young man," says Max. "It all depends on how you spin it. I agree if they come out and say everyone is to be given an ID Chip, so the government can keep tabs on you every moment of every day, then yes, there'd be a rebellion. It's an invasion of privacy."

Someone from wardrobe steps in, holding up two tailored suit jackets. "Plain or Pin stripes sir?" asks the guy from Wardrobe.

"Pin stripes of course!" says Max. "Are you trying to make me look like a cunt or what?!"

"They'll be in your dressing room Mr. Masters," replies the Wardrobe guy, nodding apologetically.

Max takes a sip of his cappuccino and continues his rant as a hair stylist attempts to fix his crown. Max doesn't exactly make their life easy, not holding still for a second.

"If they're clever," continues Max, "They'll lead up to it with a story of a missing child, thought to have been kidnapped by a pedophile. Well, if that child had a RFID implant they could track them down in minutes. No distraught parents, their lives ruined forever. The kid would be safe and sound, the sicko behind bars. If they spin the story like that, work the angle, bust out the PR machine, hell I'd be all for the ID chip. It's all about spin... Tell the big wigs in parliament we'll cut it out of the DVD release but I'm gonna want to be on the Queen's New Year's Honours list."

The production assistant can't quite believe what he's hearing.

"You think anything you see on the box is real?!" says Max. "Even the things portrayed as real like the news and documentaries have an agenda. A purpose. It's manipulation of the masses. Mind control and entertainment all at the same time."

Max tosses his cappuccino in a rubbish bin, missing the target and spilling coffee all over the floor. Crew members instantly dart over to clean up the mess and win Max's admiration.

"You really want me to say that?" asks the runner. "Did I stutter? No... jog on and earn your fucking pay cheque!"

An intern motions to get their two cents in, but Max's Personal Assistant shoves her way in front with her notepad armed and ready.

"Mr. Masters?" she says.

"Yes, speak to me Veronica." Max retorts.

"Actually it's Ashley sir."

"What happened to the last girl?"

"Veronica had a nervous breakdown. Your last assistant Monique is suing you for sexual harassment."

"That was the spotty one right?"

"Erm, I guess so."

Max laughs. "She'd be fucking lucky."

"Mr. Masters," says the Personal Assistant in a serious tone. "The sister is kicking up a fuss again. We think she keeps trying to warn him. Security caught her trying to bribe her way onto set as an extra."

"Remind her of the contract," Max snorts back unconcerned.

"She's going to the press with..."

"...with what?" he interrupts. "Nothing. That's what. Silly bitch. Slip her an extra ten grand. She causes trouble and there'll be a breaking news scandal about her family plastered over every network before she can even get a chance to refuse to comment. The man behind the things you see on TV... He's God almighty with the devil's temper."

"She doesn't want the money," says the P.A.

"What is she, a fucking hippy?!" Max replies.

"I guess she..."

"Let's just ditch the bitch. I don't want her miserable face clogging up my beautiful creation anyway."

Max Masters paces though the set as crew members sweep up the ticker tape. The stage lighting is off and the bleachers are empty.

Max pats a chubby employee on the back as he passes, tossing a comment back over his shoulder.

"You're doing a good job there buddy."

The employee lights up with pride. Max and his entourage keep moving. As soon as the employee's out of earshot, Max turns to his Personal Assistant and says, "Plant a bunch of stationery in fattie's locker, so we can sack the fella before he has a heart attack on set and sends my insurance premiums through the fucking roof."

The Personal Assistant begrudgingly scribbles down the order, her morals being thrown out the window to advance her career.

Max Masters enters the studio gallery and approaches his editor.

"Nice job on those highlight packages," says Max.

"Cheers," the Editor replies. "We've prepped the reset, he's already awake."

Max takes a chair next to the editor. A make up girl fusses over Max's complexion but he swats her away.

"Mr. Masters?" asks a sales Executive.

"Speak!" says Max.

"Just got off the phone with Pepsi. They want to know if they can place vending machines in the warehouse set?"

"Would terrorists acquire can machines?" questions Max.

"Guess they could have been left over from when the warehouse was in business," suggests the Editor.

"Have Pepsi send me some figures!" orders Max.

"Yes sir, right away," says the sales Exec. "Also a car company asked if we could include their new line of Chevrolets?"

"Can we have a prototype to blow up?" replies Max intrigued.

"I'll ask," replies the sales Exec, hurrying off to get to business.

In walks the actress who had played Kristian's Ex Wife. She's wearing sunglasses indoors with a cute little pampered dog in her Versace handbag. Think classic diva stereotype.

"Hey Max," she yells. "Tell your production monkeys backstage to keep quiet during the basement scene. They almost ruined it."

"Will do," he replies.

"And when are we gonna talk about getting me more screen time?"

"Have your agent call the office."

Max snaps his fingers to get the unbridled attention of his Personal Assistant and tells her, "Make a note in my diary. We'll set up a meeting."

Satisfied the actress struts away. The second her back's turned, Max gestures to his P.A, swiping an imaginary blade across his throat. The Personal Assistant crosses out the last diary entry and exits.

"It's interesting how he doesn't always make the same decision," says the Editor. "You know, from a purely scientific point of view."

"Science Schmience... As long as the ratings are good my Friend," shrugs Max Masters. "Personally, I couldn't care less."

"You know, I reckon he'll shoot the cop sooner or later," says the Editor. "When he went for Bullhorn last time, I thought he'd finally snapped. What if he actually embraces the evil terrorist character?"

"The audience would never see that coming. Could be a good twist."

The studio gallery consists of a giant bank of video monitors.

Each displays Kristian on a different run, going through various scenes. He's relived that story over and over.

During one of the replays Kristian is running away from the Vultures in the initial town square confrontation. In another he opens the briefcase full of cash in the hotel room and starts celebrating, while in the next one he jolts back horrified. In a fourth run through, Kristian fights with the Waiter in the hotel room, while in another replay he tries to hang himself after finding the CIA agent's body. A number of crew members dash in before he can be strangled.

"Which background history theme are we going with this time?" asks the editor. "Rapist, animal torturer or serial killer?"

"I think we'll stick with the mass murderer thing caused by his wife cheating with his brother. See what happens twice in a row."

"You don't want to switch it up to being his abusive father or kiddy-fiddling high school gym teacher?"

"The child molester thing didn't really go down too well with the network."

"Are we going with the transsexual thing again?"

"Yeah, let's risk it. I'm interested to see if he'll fall for it again."

"People trafficking, prostitution, selling human organs on the black market or underground cock fighting?"

"I'll get back to you on that one."

"You don't think that's all a little implausible," says a nervous intern.

"How's this for implausible?!" says Max. "Some virgin gives birth to a child that grows up to turn H.2.O into liquor, heal the sick with his touch, gets brutally murdered then comes back to fucking life. Sounds pretty far fetched right…? Most famous story of all time, millions upon millions have eaten it up without so much as battering an eyelid."

"That's kinda different!"

"Bollocks it is!" says Max. "The audience will swallow anything I fucking feed them, get on their knees and beg me for more. I tell them what to like. I tell them what to hate. The only free will they have is with a remote in their hands. I'm the puppet master. The viewing public are my sheep!"

145

The Intern is lost for words.

"Who the fuck are you anyway?" asks Max.

"I'm one of your new interns sir," he replies.

"Well go and make yourself useful."

The intern paces away leaving Max and his Editor in peace. On the live TV monitor, Kristian has already unlocked the briefcase full of cash and just discovered the gun in the bedside draw. He brings the weapon up to his skull.

"No," says Max. "Not another early one!"

Kristian thinks twice. He pockets the gun, takes the briefcase and is out the door and headed for the elevators.

"That's my boy!" says Max as a smile props up the corners of mouth.

On screen the Indian Girl is right on cue and hot on Kristian's tail.

A production Assistant comes up to Max and the Editor.

"Excuse me Max," says the Assistant.

"Mr. Masters!" Max quickly corrects.

"Sorry... Mr. Masters," apologies the Assistant. "The auditions for next season are underway. The casting director has picked out his favourite six and they're waiting for you in the green room."

"Are these auditions to be cast members or contestants?" enquires Max.

"Contestants!" the Assistant replies. "We had an alarmingly high number of hopeful entrants for the next series."

"Okay good, I'll be right with you."

Max stands and smoothes down his designer suit, checking to make sure his tie is perfectly in place.

"How do I look?" Max asks his Editor.

"Like a star Mr. Masters," he replies.

"I better get my name on the Walk Of Fame for this show!"

Max turns and walks towards the green room. An eager line of contestants waiting.

"The things people will do for their fifteen minutes!" he smirks.

Max strolls away, leaving the gallery behind.

On the live monitor, Kristian is in the elevator, sweating and panic stricken. He notices the surveillance camera filming above and stares straight down the lens.

The editor's mobile rings and he steps away from his desk to take the call, not paying attention to the live monitor as Kristian holds his glare for an extra long moment. The fear in Kristian's face seems to fade. It's almost as though he's looking deep into the soul of the surveillance camera.

Does he remember?

The Editor returns as Kristian snaps out of his trance and continues with his journey.

The Editor begins to make notes. Not just on Kristian though. The gallery in front of him contains an enormous never ending wall, stacked with TV monitors, each displaying a different contestant living out a challenging story line shot by CCTV camera angles.

Dozens of wannabee reality stars stuck in high octane scenarios.

The show has become an out of control cancer. A multi-million pound empire.

The future of reality TV.